A MOST UNUSUAL ELECTION

A NOVEL ABOUT A PRESIDENTIAL RACE

WENDELL B. WILL

IUNIVERSE, INC.
NEW YORK   BLOOMINGTON

A Most Unusual Election
A Novel About A Presidential Race

*This is a work of fiction. All of the characters, names, incidents,
organizations, and dialogue in this novel are either the products
of the author's imagination or are used fictitiously.*

iUniverse books may be ordered through booksellers or by contacting:

*iUniverse
1663 Liberty Drive
Bloomington, IN 47403
www.iuniverse.com
1-800-Authors (1-800-288-4677)*

*ISBN: 978-1-4401-7217-5 (sc)
ISBN: 978-1-4401-7218-2 (ebk)*

Printed in the United States of America

iUniverse rev. date: 11/2/2009

Other Books by Wendell B. Will

Not By Bread Alone

Mercy on Trial

Selected Short Stories

PREFACE

Fifteen years have gone by with no further terrorist attacks. All but a token of coalition forces have been withdrawn from Iraq and Afghanistan. Bin Laden had not been heard of in years and has probably died from natural causes somewhere in the mountains of Pakistan. The world is at peace. The long nightmare initiated by September 11, 2001 seems to most to be as distant as the upheavals caused by Adolph Hitler's Germany and Japan of 1941. However, unknown to the world a new threatening al Qaeda has arisen on a remote Pacific islaind.

CHAPTER ONE

It was 6:00 A.M. in Washington, D.C. Still in his robe, Mark Stevens was now 60, tall and with totally white hair. He was considered to be an even more good-looking man than he was when younger. He retrieved the *Washington Post* from outside his Georgetown townhouse. It was late October and the nation's capital was having its first cold snap. It would be three years in January since Mark had moved from San Francisco, but he still was not acclimated to the extremes of Washington weather. The hot summer humidity had been brutal and he dreaded the raw, heavy cold of the coming winter.

"Good morning, Mr. Stevens, your breakfast is waiting."

"Thank you, Jorge," Mark answered.

Jorge Prado had come to Washington with Mark from San Francisco where he had supervised the staffs at Mark's residences—the Nob Hill condominium, the mansion in Hillsborough, and the Pebble Beach retreat. Jorge was slim and of medium height. Although over the years Jorge had become as much a companion to Mark as an employee, he had retained his custom of wearing a dark jacket, tie and gray trousers.

When he was confirmed by the Senate, Mark had bought the restored Georgetown townhouse from a Democratic senator, defeated for office in the voting that had increased the Republican majorities in Congress and had kept the White House in Republican hands.

Since Mark never returned to Georgetown until late evening, breakfast was the only meal he ate at his townhouse. When he entertained dignitaries, he often used Washington's Cosmos Club.

Mark opened the newspaper and was startled by the headline above the left column:

STEVENS MAY RESIGN

Mark came in from the cold, put on his half-glasses, and stood in the narrow paneled foyer, reading.

> *Reliable sources report that Secretary of the Treasury, Mark Stevens, long known to have serious differences with President Knox, is contemplating resigning as early as his meeting today with the President.*

Mark was irritated. How did the *Post* know about this morning's scheduled meeting? And where had this resignation rumor come from? Admittedly, he had occasionally considered the possibility of resigning, but he contained his frustration with President Knox and had told no one. Until now he had thought resignation would be his choice alone, and not the President's. Obviously, the White House had leaked the story. Mark felt the leak would not be without the knowledge of the President himself. Perhaps Knox was laying the groundwork for Mark's resignation.

Angered, Mark continued reading the *Post*:

> *Stevens, who is listed by Forbes magazine as the world's second richest man, and never one to keep his opinions to himself, freely spoke in Tuesday's House committee hearing. Stevens, a former Rhodes scholar and an internationally recognized financial expert, was particularly critical of Federal Reserve chairman Rosenthal and his tight money policies. President Knox, who upon his election nearly three years ago appointed Rosenthal, has publicly supported the Federal Reserve's interest rate hikes. However, Stevens testified that the increased rates might lead to a recession. But the real bombshell that rocked Washington exploded when, under prodding by maverick Representative Claude Raymond (D. Michigan), Stevens asserted his belief that, as was the case prior to September 11, 2001, the country and the government had once again gone to sleep over the renewed threat of terrorism. It has been rumored that Stevens has privately warned the President that a serious terrorist threat has again reared . . .*

The story continued past the first page, but Mark read no more. He ignored his waiting breakfast and angrily climbed the stairs two at a time to dress for the day and the meeting with the President, a meeting that Knox's chief of staff had requested only yesterday. Tensions with Knox had been at their worst lately, and Mark had suspected the meeting would not be routine.

Mark dressed in one of the richly patterned, dark Brioni suits he had brought from San Francisco. He chose his boldest red tie rather than the conservative "Washington stripes" he usually wore to White House meetings. The red tie fit his frame of mind this morning. He would not be intimidated by Knox's well-known aura of power, President of the United States, or not.

Jorge was waiting in front in the old Rolls-Royce limousine. Mark loved the Rolls Phantom. He kept a right hand drive duplicate car at his London home. The two cars were his first purchases after he had become wealthy, when he took his investment banking firm public 30 odd years ago. He enjoyed the elegance of the old cars more than any other possessions his wealth had brought him.

As Jorge drove toward the Treasury Department, Mark was both fuming and puzzled. He knew the President could be a devious politician, but when he accepted the Treasury post the then President-elect had told him he could speak his mind on policy issues as long as disagreements had first been privately discussed. True to their understanding, Mark had often discussed his disagreements with the President, but had kept them private. Neither the press nor the cabinet knew that Mark had, in fact, warned the President several times that he had it on nearly irrefutable authority that the terrorist threat, although once subdued, again seriously threatened the country.

The warnings had come from Christina Bagliani, owner and publisher of the Italian newspaper, *Il Verita*.

Christina had inherited the newspaper from her husband and had built the periodical into a respected international daily. When Mark had been a college student at Cal he and Christina had been lovers, but Christina had chosen to marry the much older Bagliani, whose substantial newspaper holdings included *Il Verita*.

Christina and Mark had remained close over the years, especially after Mark's wife had been killed in the hotel fire and Christina's husband had died. Several times of late, Christina had telephoned Mark with warnings that her investigative reporters were engaged in uncovering a serious terrorist plot. Although her investigation was incomplete the threat appeared real, and Mark had warned the President. He was dismayed and puzzled by Knox's casual attitude toward the information.

As Jorge guided the large Rolls through Washington traffic, Mark thought back on how, in the beginning, Knox had given him unqualified support. At his Senate confirmation hearings, Mark had refused to sell his stock in The Stevens Company, raising a mild furor. But the President had personally brokered an agreement with the committee chairman that enabled Mark's confirmation as Treasury Secretary. Mark agreed not to be involved in the management of the company he had founded, but he would not have to sell his stock. Knox had wanted Mark's independent views and, more than that, wanted to give the appearance to the electorate of a President open to dissent.

The President-elect had even joked in an early press conference about the flap over Mark's beloved Rolls-Royce. "Do you want the second richest man in the country to be seen riding around Washington in a two-seater bicycle with his chauffeur in front?" Knox was good at charming the press. That charm had made the difference in his narrow election victory.

But something had happened since those early days. The President continued to be affable with Mark. That was his way. But Knox's underlying attitude had changed. Initially the President had consulted Mark about a wide variety of matters, but the invitations to golf had lessened and finally stopped. Presidential phone calls seeking advice had all but ceased. Mark had wondered if Christina's warnings had struck the President as ill-founded and whether the President had lost confidence in him.

As the Rolls arrived at Treasury, Mark wondered if at today's meeting the President would ask for his resignation as the *Post* had speculated. There was no telling. Knox was a political enigma.

As was Mark's custom, he walked the short distance from Treasury to the White House for the 10:00 A.M. meeting. The weather was slightly warmer, but the sun was still behind the cloud cover. He acknowledged the security guard who waved him up the driveway. The White House usher opened the front door as Mark arrived.

"Hello, Mr. Secretary," greeted the usher as he took Mark's topcoat. "It's a bit cold today, sir."

"Reminds me of San Francisco, Frank. How's that new grandson of yours?" Mark asked with a smile.

"Fine, sir. Just fine. Thank you for asking."

Most visitors did not go to the west wing by way of the White House North entrance, but it was a delightful custom for Mark. It reminded him of his first time in the historic mansion. It had been when Nixon was President, before the Watergate scandal broke. Treasury Secretary John Connally had invited Mark to a dinner meeting with the President. An international crisis had arisen over the threatened run on the U.S. gold stored in Ft. Knox and Connally had been impressed by a speech Mark had given concerning the theory of monetary policy that Mark had refined while a student at Oxford.

The usher stood nearby as Mark nostalgically walked to the door of the East Room. Nixon and Connally had called the dinner meeting with a small group of foreign currency experts to discuss the gold crisis. Mark stood at the door remembering. Even then, despite being barely 30 and in the awesome presence of the President of the United States, Mark had been outspoken. The not-yet-disgraced President had invited him to a meeting at Camp David that had resulted in the new international financial system still in use today. Since then, Mark had been invited to the White House by every Republican President. Even the Democrat Clinton had asked Mark to lend his influence on the passage of NAFTA.

Accompanied by the usher, Mark reverently walked through the grand White House cross hall with its columns. He paused at the portrait of a pensive John Kennedy. He remembered as a Rhodes scholar at Oxford, hearing the news of the young President's assassination. November 22, 1963. The same chill he always felt at the remembrance went up his body as he made his way toward the executive wing.

It was exactly 10:00 o'clock when Mark arrived at the desk of the President's secretary, Sherri. No matter that Mark had been in the oval office many times, that he had made many significant observations to powerful people, and had made decisions involving billions of dollars, Mark was aware of the childhood belief still lurking deep inside him.

"Son, there are Big Shots and there are people like you and me," his father had repeatedly preached.

"There's a ditch wider than the whole damn Grand Canyon between them and us. And don't you forget it. Ever."

Mark smiled at himself as he remembered his father's red-necked voice. He thought he had put those words behind him years ago, but obviously they were still there, waiting their chance. Why else would they pop into his mind just before meeting with the President? Apparently a man could never fully shake his father's beliefs. He recalled reading how the outwardly cool John Kennedy's hands used to tremble while making speeches. The years had taught Mark that although the old voice of self-doubt would never be completely silent, his task was to choose the path of confidence. And that was exactly what he would do in this meeting with Knox.

"Good morning, Mr. Secretary," said Sherri. "The President is on the telephone with the Chinese Premier, but he wants you to go on in." Sherri was an attractive brunette. Her high cheekbones reminded Mark of Lady Mavis Ashley, his mentor in England years ago. He had been tempted to invite Sherri to dinner, but she was the President's secretary. He was too busy to date anyway.

President Stuart Knox was behind his desk in the oval office, talking. He motioned to Mark to sit on one of the two sofas. It was obvious that the slow process of translation was irritating to the President. "All well and good, then. Sometime in January," the President concluded. "We'll make your first trip to the United States a memorable one. Goodbye, sir. Oh, and bring your heavy coat. It can be just as cold in Washington as in Beijing."

Knox waited several moments for the translators to finish and hung up. Standing, he turned to Mark. The President was a trim good-looking man who had been 51 when he was elected. He, too, wore a dark, expensive suit and a bold tie. "I don't know what that son-of-a-bitch is up to, but I can tell you it's not good." The President walked around his desk and sat on the twin sofa opposite Mark. Knox exuded supreme confidence. In contrast to Mark's completely white hair, the President still showed no sign of gray. Even as a Republican, Knox had won fifty-two percent of the female vote. The President was a winner as a politician, Mark had to agree.

"I'll tell you what they want," Mark answered. "They're Chinese. They want even more trade. Simple as that. And your policies are cutting them off at the knees."

"For the life of me, Mark, I still don't understand your wanting more trade with China. They're taking jobs from American workers. Paying pitiful wages. Their human rights are no better than they were five hundred years ago." The President lit a cigarette. The public didn't know he smoked. For that matter they didn't know about his girl friend. Mark knew, but if the First Lady knew, she kept it to herself.

"We're talking international trade here, Stuart. We're not talking about the condition of the Chinese workers." Mark never called the President by his first name when others were present, but he'd be damned if he'd call him

"Mr. President" in private. After all, Knox's main quality for the Presidency was being a good-looking master politician with a mediocre mind. Early on, Mark had vowed that it would be "Stuart" in private.

"Mark, I'm not talking trade barriers."

"Dammit, Stuart, you certainly are. Maybe not tariffs in terms of import taxes, but when you try to impose American standards on a foreign country, you're talking trade barriers as surely as old-fashioned tariffs. I remember Henry Kissinger saying years ago that Americans show unabashed effrontery when as a two hundred-plus year old country we try to force a five thousand year-old country to run its affairs the way we want. We're still doing it. Trying to."

"But we can't just sit by and let them pay their workers a fraction of what our workers get. Oh, I know, you say the Chinese are glad for the work. But, Mark, what about our workers and their jobs? What about our unions?"

Mark knew he hadn't been summoned to the White House to discuss trade with China. Knox was really just making conversation before he got to the real point of the meeting. Mark would play the game until the President was ready.

"Look, the unions aren't going to support a Republican, no matter what you do," Mark continued. "The answer is having a more productive worker—helping them to get good, more productive jobs. Even Clinton saw that. You remember NAFTA."

"Yeah, Clinton was another Oxford man." Knox was referring to Clinton, as well as Mark, both being Rhodes scholars. Oxford men were usually free traders. "We've been over this time and time again. You may be right, but people who buy Chinese-made underwear don't vote for cheaper underwear. Union members vote their jobs, dammit."

Knox walked to his desk and crushed out his cigarette.

"Mark, I only knew you by reputation when I was elected."

This morning's headline flashed across Mark's mind. *STEVENS MAY RESIGN.* Finally! Here it comes, he thought.

The President continued. "I knew you knew more about economics than any other on the short list for Treasury." The President turned and looked at Mark. "Mark, I never told you this, but Harry thought you were too opinionated and wouldn't be able to go along with me. The political ramifications, you know." Harry was Harold Manning, Knox's chief of staff.

"Perhaps Harry was right." Mark retorted. "After all, you and I come from different worlds. I'm used to making my own decisions. I don't like worrying about what people might think."

"You know I can't behave that way," Knox answered. "I certainly wish I could. When I was first a congressman and then as a senator I had to compromise all the time. That's what politicians have to do."

"Stuart, I can compromise. I've made many a deal—"

The President interrupted Mark. "I'm talking about real compromise. Compromising principle. I don't think you can do that. Take this China trade thing. The truth is you're probably right about it. I'm certainly no economist. But listen, Mark, there's no way I can buy into your theories in the real world of politics. I want a second term. And your ideas aren't going to get me any second term."

"And my warning about the terrorist threat? What about that?"

"That's a bunch of crap. Your newspaper friend is way off base." Obviously Knox was referring to Christina. Knox certainly knew very well that Christina was more than a "friend." Knox was known to keep himself up-to-date on the personal lives of every high ranking official.

"There's no terrorist threat," Knox continued. "I've had it checked out by the CIA. Yeah, I admit, there's some activity off Malaysia, or someplace, by some crackpots, but if I raised the alarm every time some two-bit crazies somewhere in the world foamed at the mouth about the United States, people would think I was the crazy one. The country just isn't interested the way it once was."

Mark stood angrily facing the President across his desk. "And if you did raise the alarm, you think your chances for a second term would go out the window, isn't that so? The truth is that's the main reason why you won't take me seriously. It's damn inconvenient with the voters."

Knox's face turned red. "You're out of line Mr. Secretary. I suggest you sit down." The President had never called him Mr. Secretary. "These people your friend tells you about are no more of a threat than those nuts who march up and down in Idaho. I'm not going to ask Congress for billions to fight what your alarmist girl friend thinks is a serious threat." Knox was very angry.

But Mark, just as angry, ignored the Presidential order and remained standing facing the President. "That's the difference between you and me. A second term would never be that important to me." Mark paused and then backed away from the desk to the sofa.

Knox turned and looked out the window behind his desk. He stood there gathering himself, staring at the gray weather. It seemed to Mark that the impasse would last indefinitely.

Finally the President turned. His anger had cooled. Mark had decided to resume his seat on the sofa. "Don't you understand?" the President entreated. "It's important to the country that I be re-elected. If the Democrats get control, all my work—your work too—goes down the drain. If your friend is right about this terrorist crap, we'll find out about it soon enough."

Mark was still annoyed. "Trouble is, Stuart, almost every President you could name pointed towards a second term from the time he was first elected. They all did. 'It's for the good of the country,' they always say. Well it's not for the good of the country at all. It's their lust for power. They all love the power."

"Dammit, Mark, that's not true! At least of me." Knox jammed out his just-lit second cigarette. "I could make two or three million a year practicing law and sitting on my ass. I don't need a second term."

"Money's not the point, Stuart," Mark countered. "You're not exempt. Power is in the blood of every politician I've ever met."

"Ambition has its place even in politics."

"Maybe, but not ambition just for power. Ambition to accomplish things. That's different. I'll buy that. But not blind ambition for power."

"I can see we're never going to settle this." Knox walked around his desk looking at Mark. "Mark, I want to ask you something."

"I figured you did and it isn't about trade with China or my philosophy about politicians. I read the *Post* this morning."

"I'm sorry about the *Post*. I don't know where they got that resignation stuff."

"Oh, come on, Stuart. If you want my resignation just ask for it. There's no need to plant stories."

"Mark, I didn't leak the story. I'll admit I told Harry—"

"Told Harry what?"

"Harry and I had a talk once. You know about your friend's terrorist threat stuff. Harry's the only one—"

"So you did tell Harry. You know damn well Harry can't keep his mouth shut. He's your chief of leaks. He's got to be the one behind the tip to Congressman Raymond. Dammit, Stuart, my warning was supposed to be confidential. Your ears only. Okay, maybe the CIA. But that was it. When Raymond was badgering me at yesterday's hearing, I wondered where he got his information. I should have known it was Harry's doing."

"Listen, I've the right to discuss everything with my Chief of Staff. You shouldn't have answered that Congressman's questions." The President raised his voice. "What's his name? I keep forgetting."

"Raymond," Mark answered. "You know Raymond's always looking for a headline. Well, he got it."

"He baited you."

"Maybe I should have kept my mouth shut, but terrorism is a serious issue. The whole damn country has fallen asleep again. Sure, we thought we had it stamped out, but its come back. There's going to be another attack. It's just a matter of time."

"There's not going to be another attack. We keep on top of these things."

"We thought we were on top of things back in '01. But we weren't. We've fallen asleep again. We had a few victories and things got quiet. But now we're back in a state of pure complacency. Naive complacency. This country is asking for trouble and you're not doing a damn thing about it."

"I don't mind your raising the issue privately with me. But you should have told that asshole Raymond to buzz off."

"What was I supposed to say?"

"You could have lied, dammit."

"So you want me to lie. Is that it?"

"Well, at least you could have refused to answer. Executive privilege. Anything." Knox paused. "Look, it hurts me politically for you to be disagreeing in public all the time. I swear sometimes you think you're the President, not me. Mark, you're off base on this one."

"I was testifying before a House committee. Under oath. 'Be a good boy and shut your mouth.' That's what you're telling me isn't it? I didn't take this job to be a figurehead. That was our deal. Who needs a job like that? Cabinet post or no cabinet post."

"Mark, there's only a few months until the primaries start and then the election." The President's tone was conciliatory. If you want to resign, all I ask is you wait until after. I know we get pissed off at one another, but I need your support in the election."

"You want me to resign, but not yet? Is that it?" Mark made no effort to hide his displeasure.

"I don't want you to resign at all. Having you in my cabinet could mean my re-election."

"And after the election?"

"You could either quit or stay on. You're obviously upset. We both are. I'd keep you on, if you wanted."

"And if I stayed on, you wouldn't pay any attention to me. That's about it, isn't it?"

The President made a move toward the door. He was ending the conference.

"It's nothing personal, Mark. I admire you. If I had your money, I would probably never have gotten into politics in the first place. Who needs it? It's times like this that I hate the whole damned thing."

The President did not offer to shake Mark's hand as they parted.

"So long, Sherri," Mark said to the secretary, covering his anger.

"See you soon, Mr. Stevens," Sherri responded with her upbeat tone.

I wonder, Mark thought absently as he left. *I wonder if I'll ever be here again.*

CHAPTER TWO

As Mark angrily strode from the White House for the Treasury Building, a saying from his favorite President, Thomas Jefferson, came to mind. "When a man aspires to political office," Jefferson had mused, "he becomes no longer true to himself. His mind becomes twisted in justification of his desire for power."

What Jefferson had observed in himself as well as others was the same trait that Stuart Knox had just exhibited—continued power was more important than leadership. Human nature had never changed from the early primitive chieftains to Presidents of the United States.

Instead of returning to his office, Mark walked swiftly to the Treasury garage where his Ferrari awaited. This morning's events had stirred a vital energy within him. The last thing he would do was spend the day behind his desk. For years Mark had kept a sports car in addition to his Rolls. He tossed his top coat, suit jacket and tie on the passenger seat and eased into the firm, yet sumptuous, driver's seat. He had not started the speedy 12-cylinder machine in nearly a month, but its distinctive whine came to immediate life. With its 600 plus horsepower, the red car yearned to rocket Mark forward. It only awaited its master's command.

As Mark turned onto busy Pennsylvania Avenue, Thomas Jefferson was still on his mind. He wondered if fate were ever to make him President, he would be any different. Or would he succumb to the power lust of Stuart Knox—succumb to the temptation Jefferson had observed. Perhaps it was arrogant for any man to think he might be different.

Mark did not know where he wanted to drive, but he knew he wanted it to be away from Washington and fast. He ducked around a slower car, loving the mellow sound exuded by the 12 cylinders with its exhaust receptive to the gas pedal. He knew one thing for certain. A President should get things done and not succumb to the need to remain in power. A President should lead the country toward controversial goals. Free trade. A vigorous foreign policy. Lower taxes. Maybe a flat tax. Get the government out of the way so that business could create new jobs. Above all, smash this new terrorist threat.

Upon crossing the bridge to Virginia, Mark was driving well over the speed limit. Suddenly it dawned on him that he was steering the beast of a car toward Jefferson's home, Monticello. Why on Earth was he driving deep into Virginia? It would be almost dark when he would get there. It was a crazy idea, but he didn't care. The argument with Knox had put him in the mood for not giving a damn.

Thomas Jefferson's architectural masterpiece was magnificent in the fall late afternoon light. The leaves on the trees had turned, but had not yet fallen. Mark had found inspiration at Monticello several previous times.

Today, there were a number of tourists as he made his way through the familiar rooms. He marveled again at the many talents of the man who had accomplished so much in his illustrious career. Supposedly John Kennedy had remarked, after a meeting with a group of intellectuals, that there had not been such an assemblage of brainpower at the White House since the third President had dined alone.

Later, when Mark finished his tour of the unique home with its historical aura, he stood alone facing Jefferson's obelisk in the small graveyard. He read again the inscription—an inscription composed by Jefferson himself.

Here was buried
Thomas Jefferson

Author of the Declaration of American Independence
Of the Statute of Virginia's Religious Freedom
& Father of the University of Virginia

Odd, but perhaps very telling, that Jefferson had made no reference to being President of the nation he had co-founded.

Mark wondered if Jefferson could have been elected in the 21st century. Probably not. Jefferson had rebelled against an intrusive federal government. His arguments with the Federalists, such as Hamilton, had led to the two party system. Today people wanted more government than ever. Giant bureaucracies to solve every problem. Doing the job badly and spending far too much money doing it. Money raised by taxes that destroyed people's incentive to care for themselves. No, Mark concluded. Jefferson would not be elected today, but probably not even Hamilton would because the government had become so intrusive.

As Mark stood in near darkness before the grave marker, he wondered. What if Jefferson were alive? Would the great sage urge Mark to resign as Secretary of Treasury, or would he advise staying on and doing what he could to foster his beliefs? After all Jefferson had resigned in mid-term when he was Secretary of State. And the President with whom he had disagreed had been George Washington, not the often-inept Stuart Knox. He wished Jefferson could ride back with him in the Ferrari. What a conversation they would have!

It was after midnight when Mark arrived at Georgetown. He felt he should be nearing a decision about resigning, but he did not know what it might be.

Jorge had left a note on the table.

> *Mr. Stevens. There's a sandwich in the refrigerator.*

Mark flipped on the TV as he ate the sandwich in his den. But his mind was not on what he was watching. An hour had passed when he turned off the TV and went upstairs. Sitting on the edge of his bed, he doubted if he could get to sleep. Finally, he asked aloud, "*Tell me, Mr. Jefferson. Should I quit or stay on?*

By dawn Mark had finished his longhand letter:

> *Dear Mr. President, while serving as your Secretary of the Treasury has been a challenge and an honor, I have decided that it is time for me to return to private*

life. My resignation shall be effective November 10th.

Very truly yours,

Mark thought for a moment and then signed the letter. It would be on the President's desk in the morning.

It was the next morning. Mark had allowed time for the President to read the letter of resignation. Mark had called a press conference at the Treasury Department. He wanted to make his resignation public before Knox or his staff could put their spin on the parting of the ways.

Only half a dozen correspondents were in the pressroom. No hint had been given that anything other than routine announcements would be made. Only the pool television camera was present as Mark stood at the lectern.

"Ladies and Gentlemen, an hour ago I sent my letter of resignation to President Knox. Copies are being handed to you. I will answer a few questions."

It took several seconds for the group to grasp what had been said, but then: "Mr. Secretary, it has been well known that you disagree with President Knox on many issues. What do you think is the most important?"

"I have tried to keep my disagreements private. That is the way it should be, between the President and me."

"But, sir, you are no longer in the cabinet. Shouldn't you let your views be known?"

"I'm eager to return to private life, but I will mention one or two points that I feel especially strongly about. Points that, as a private citizen, I expect I will work towards solving. First, I believe the threat from secret terrorist organizations is very real. I feel we, as a nation, have again become complacent. And second, ever since the Greenspan era we have been relying far too heavily on the Fed's power to raise and lower interest rates to control our economy. It's like cleaning a fine watch with a sledge hammer."

Then, Mark felt he was making a mistake in speaking out this way.

"But I've said enough," he concluded, making a move to leave.

"Mr. Secretary, one more question. Just now you sounded like a candidate. Will you run for President?"

"Absolutely not. I have always been at my happiest when I've been running my businesses. I intend to return to that joyful life. I'll speak out on public issues, as I always have, certainly. But politics is not for me. I have no talent for politics. I'll leave that to others."

As Mark walked off the podium one last question was shouted.

"Will you support President Knox if he decides to run again?"

Mark was out of sight by the time the questioner had finished.

The President was in his small office near the oval office. His Chief of Staff had replayed Mark's appearance. "Mark my words, Harry. Mark my words. He'll end up running against me."

It was raining in Georgetown when the plastic-wrapped *Post* landed on Mark's front steps early the next morning. The beads of water nearly obscured the headline.

STEVENS RESIGNS DENIES BID FOR PRESIDENT BUT SOME ARE SKEPTICAL

But the newspaper would remain lying in the rain. Mark's jet had taken off for California before dawn.

CHAPTER THREE

It had been two months since Mark had resigned as Secretary of the Treasury. He had returned to San Francisco from Washington with new enthusiasm. Originally he was excited by the idea of plunging back into his investment banking business. After all it was his business life that had brought him such great satisfaction in the past.

But he was disappointed. David Greenbaum, whom he had elevated from President to Chairman when he left for Washington, was running the business as well as he, himself, could do. Mark was forced to recognize that he was not needed. Perhaps he had made an impulsive decision leaving government. He did miss making significant decisions.

Cold heavy fog obscured most of the San Francisco Bay as he breakfasted in his Nob Hill condominium. With nothing challenging to do, he felt as dreary as the weather.

Jorge answered the ring of the telephone. "It's Mrs. Swenson for you, sir. She's crying." Mrs. Swenson was the live-in companion of Mark's mother.

Mark picked up the telephone from the breakfast table. "Yes, Mrs. Swenson. What's the trouble? Is it mother?" Mark's mother, Amanda Stevens, had suffered a stroke shortly after Mark had moved to Washington. Through therapy, her thinking and speaking capacities had largely returned, although she still was confined to a wheel chair and dependent upon Mrs. Swenson. Even with her disability, Amanda remained the driving force behind the sanctuary she had founded for abused women and children near Sonoma, an hour's drive north of San Francisco.

"I'm sorry, Mr. Stevens, but I do have bad news. Very bad. Your mother . . . " With that her sobbing increased.

"What is it? Has she had another stroke?"

"No, Mr. Stevens I'm afraid your mother passed away. Less than an hour ago."

Deep in thought Mark sat in the front pew of the church of his youth. He was barely listening to the minister eulogizing his mother.

"Amanda Stevens was known for her good works here in Sonoma," said the elderly clergyman. Reverend Mitchell had been young and vigorous when Mark graduated from Cal Berkeley and left to study at Oxford 40 years ago.

"When Amanda inherited the winery and vineyard from her employer, Sonoma's own Antonio Movelli, she could have lived in the mansion where she had been little more than a servant." The Reverend continued: "Instead, with the aid of her son, she turned the stately building into a haven for abused women and children and continued living in her nearby cottage." The sanctuary was filled with mourners, many standing at the rear. Reverend Mitchell had come from his retirement home for the funeral.

Mark's thoughts drifted. His father's funeral had been in this church. Mark was then in his first year as a Rhodes scholar at Oxford. Jonah had suddenly died in a hotel room with one of his women. Despite his hate for his father, Mark had hurried home from England. His mother had needed his support.

Through Mark's childhood Amanda had protected Mark from Jonah. Many times she had risked another punch in the face from her hard-drinking husband so as to save her son from more of Jonah's abuse and ridicule.

Mark had never forgiven his father, even though he had come to realize the abuse had created the very unyielding drive that had made him into the billionaire perfectionist he had become.

Mark remembered his mother telling him at breakfast after Jonah's funeral: "Reverend Mitchell says that we must forgive those who have sinned against us—not for their sake, but for our own."

The young embittered Mark had answered: "But Reverend Mitchell didn't have Jonah Stevens for a father." He now knew Mitchell had been right about forgiveness, but the passage of years had only softened his hatred, not eliminated it. In truth there had been no forgiveness.

Over 50 people gathered by Amanda's open grave in the hillside of Sonoma's historic Mountain View Cemetery. "Dearly beloved, we are gathered on this rugged hillside to say a final goodbye," Reverend Mitchell began.

Mark did not want to hear the painful ceremony. He walked down the hill and stood by Pris's grave marker. "Priscilla Enfield Stevens 1945-1980." He recalled the horrible hotel fire in Las Vegas. Pris and he had decided to make a fresh start on their troubled marriage and to fly to Mexico. He would give up his passion for the beautiful Christina and rekindle his love for Pris. Bubbling with new-found joy, Pris had impulsively asked Mark to divert his jet to the distant twinkling lights of Las Vegas, instead of Mexico. The impulse had led to her death in the poisonous smoke of the hotel fire, despite Mark's heroic efforts to save her.

A mild wind, reminiscent of Pris, rustled the trees. Mark tried to imagine what his life would be like if Pris had not been killed. Would their resolve to love one another have succeeded? Would they have had children? Maybe a son and then a daughter? And what about Christina? Would he have ended his relationship with Christina as he had intended? Perhaps not, for in the years since Pris's death he saw Christina as often as he could get to Rome. How could a man love two women at the same time? But he knew it was entirely possible.

Suddenly Mark realized someone was standing beside him.

"There you are. I wondered where I'd find you." It was Rolf Williams, Mark's friend from high school days. They had been fraternity brothers at the University of California at Berkeley. Rolf had graduated law review from the university's law school, Boalt Hall, and joined a major San Francisco law firm. While Mark's limitless ambition drove him upward in investment banking, Rolf had fled the big law firm to practice law in a storefront on Sonoma's quaint central square. Through the ups and downs of their lives—romances, failed marriages, deaths, Mark's bouts with depression, business successes and failures—they had remained close friends and confidants.

"I've been looking all over for you," Rolf continued, putting his hand on Mark's shoulder. "They're nearly finished with the service. Don't you think you should be there?"

"Sorry. I've been reminiscing. You're right, Rolf. Let's go."

They climbed the steep rocky hill to Amanda's grave.

"And so we ask God to look over us," finished Reverend Mitchell. "May Amanda Stevens' memory inspire us all. We shall remember her for the rest of our days."

Mark stepped through the mourners to touch his mother's coffin.

Most of the group shook Mark's hand and mumbled a few words before they left.

"Let's go to Sally's," Mark suggested to Rolf. Sally's restaurant had been their hangout since high school days.

"I figured we would."

"But first I'd like to look at my father's grave."

They stood looking down at Jonah's headstone sticking above the plastic turf around Amanda's grave.

"Mother always wanted me to forgive him," Mark told Rolf. "I tried, but it never worked. My loathing simply became old as the years went by. What's the old saying?"

"'*Time heals all wounds*', you mean?" asked Rolf.

"Yes, that's it. I guess I healed, but it left one hell of a scar. I still think of him, jerking that tractor wheel and throwing me off like a rag doll." Mark still bore a slight limp from the tractor accident when he was young.

"Yeah, then scolding you for it." Rolf knew the story, although it had been years since Mark had mentioned it.

"He yelled at me for everything. Not one word of praise my whole goddam life."

"Maybe that's why you've always wanted a son. So you could treat him differently."

"Well, I guess it's too late for that now," Mark responded. "Let's get the hell out of here."

"Yeah. Let's go to Sally's. I'm starving."

Sally's restaurant was across Sonoma's historic square from Rolf's law office. Sally was now dead, but her daughter, Brenda, was carrying on the tradition of making the best hamburgers in the wine country. Brenda had worked with her mother and knew all the customers by name.

"Hi, boys," greeted Brenda. Sally had called them boys and, despite the fact they were Brenda's age, they were still boys to Brenda. "Do you want the window booth?"

As they sat down, Mark remembered the time they had raced across the square from Rolf's law office. "You remember that day that we—"

"Yeah. It was raining like hell," interrupted Rolf.

"We were sure soaked," Mark laughed.

"You were on your way to speak at the Bohemian Club, I remember. What did they call it?"

"The Grove. That's where I met Connally, which led to meeting Nixon." The Grove was the annual outdoor event of San Francisco's Bohemian Club, in the midst of the giant trees near the river. It was there that many of the country's business and political leaders met to have fun. Mark had given a speech about the U.S. monetary system. John Connally, Nixon's Treasury Secretary, had heard it and invited Mark to meet the President at the White House.

"It's like yesterday. I knew you when you were a mere billionaire. If you died tomorrow, you would have had an exciting life. Sometimes I envy you, my friend."

"And I envy you, Rolf. You have surely found your niche."

"Yeah, a small frog in a smaller pond," said Rolf. "Although sometimes I wish for more. And what about you? Will you ever finally find your niche?"

Mark laughed. "Knowing me, if I ever do, it'll be a niche in Mountain View Cemetery."

Rolf laughed with him. "And I'll be there too. Maybe next to you."

"Funny. We all end up in the same place." It was good for Mark to be with his friend. He was feeling better.

"You look more rested than last time I saw you," Rolf continued. "Looks like it's been good for you to get out of that Washington Beltway pressure."

"Oh, the pressure never bothered me. You know I thrive on being in the thick of things. I seem to need it, the challenges I mean. The thing that got to me was Knox. It was very frustrating." Mark paused, thinking. "I guess, we were simply on different wave lengths when it came to policy. And I never could bring him around."

"So I gathered from the news. Maybe you shouldn't have taken the job in the first place. You've never been good at being the number two guy." Both remembered Mark quitting a lucrative position while still in his 20s and starting his own investment banking firm.

"Yes, but I was Secretary of the Treasury for God's sake! Knox promised me I'd have an impact on policy." Mark looked out the window. "But it didn't turn out that way. He was President and I was not."

Rolf smiled. "Why doesn't that surprise me? Your being unhappy not being number one."

Mark chuckled. It was good to be with his old friend. He needed some relief from the past few days.

Brenda came with the hamburgers and fries. They chatted with her a bit before she left for the kitchen.

What ever happened to the guy who gave you so much trouble at Oxford? Rolf asked. "I've forgotten his name."

"Derek Hardin. Funny you should ask. Only a few months ago he tried to buy a bank in Los Angeles. He's in banking now—a billionaire several times over—a banking mogul."

"Of course, Derek Hardin. He tried to get you kicked out of Oxford. Some trumped up charge. Then, years later . . . I'll never forget that trial in San Francisco. He was trying to take over your company."

"That was one of the worst experiences of my life. He damn near succeeded too."

"But he didn't, thank God. So, did he buy the bank in L.A.?"

"No. As Secretary of Treasury I saw to it that the deal was blocked. I'd never let a crook like Derek Hardin get approval to buy an American bank. Thank goodness that was before I resigned."

"Good for you. I'll bet Hardin was pissed."

"He was buying the bank through a corporation, Global Albion, I think. But I found out he was the sole stockholder and put a stop to the deal."

They had finished their hamburgers. Mark motioned to Brenda to bring their check.

"Well, what are you going to do with yourself now?" Rolf asked when Brenda left the table.

"That's the problem. I've not been doing much of anything. Anything that matters, that is."

"Why don't you just take it easy. Live the retired rich guy's life. God knows you deserve it."

"You can only look at the Bay for so much time in a day. And I'm not much for playing backgammon at the club." He was referring to Nob Hill's exclusive Pacific Union Club across from his condominium. "Frankly it gets boring."

"And golf? What about golf?"

"I tried Pebble Beach for a week. Played most of the courses. But I don't know anyone there anymore. I'm the former Secretary of the Treasury to them—not a friend. There's never anyone to play with at Cypress Point Club. Members have to invite friends to make a foursome."

"You. Down on golf. It's hard to believe."

"Frankly, Rolf I've been depressed a lot lately. I can't seem to shake it."

"Maybe you should go see Christina. How long has it been?"

"Maybe a year. I've been so damn busy and she . . . well she's busy with *Il Verita*. The newspaper is really her whole life now." Christina had inherited the great Italian newspaper *Il Verita* from her husband and was its publisher. She had built the newspaper into a much respected international journal. Its weekend English language edition was now widely read, especially its editorials and well-researched articles. "We really haven't had much time for each other since I've been in Washington."

"Are you kidding? She'd make time for you. The flame hasn't died out for you has it?"

Mark smiled. "It's flickered a bit, but its still there. She'd never leave Italy again. Christina doesn't need a man as she did when she was young."

"Then go to London. You've got your house there. You've got friends there. Who was it who said 'When a man is tired of London he's tired of life '?"

"Johnson, I think it was. Samuel Johnson."

"Why don't you go? You could leave tonight."

"Maybe I should. I still have an open invitation to speak at Oxford—the Oxford Union."

"It would be fun. Give you a chance to spout off on some of your pet theories."

"Rodney called last week. He's all excited about some new hotel deal." Rodney Ashley was Mark's friend from his Oxford days and now his business partner in English real estate deals.

"Sure. England could be just the ticket for you to get out of your doldrums."

Mark smiled. "Maybe you're right. I could use a change of pace. I'll call and have the plane ready for London tomorrow. See what Rodney's up to."

"And one other suggestion from a old friend." Rolf shot Mark a mischievous grin."

"And just what is that?"

"If I were you I'd surely work in a trip to Rome."

When Rolf said goodbye to his friend and sat down at his law desk, he wondered about Mark. He had known very well that his old pal would never be happy playing golf or even moving from one city to another. Mark was too ambitious, too restless for that. But what should his friend do with his life? Was there any circumstance that could bring the man happiness? Ever?

Rolf sighed and resigned himself to the paperwork on his desk.

CHAPTER FOUR

Meanwhile, a continent, an ocean and eight time zones away, a black limousine approached London from the south. The passenger was returning to Britain's financial capital from a weekend at his country estate in Sussex. The man was Derek Hardin. Sixty, the same age as Mark, Hardin was a classmate and graduate of Oxford's Worcester College and a man of great wealth. Hardin controlled many banks throughout the U.K. and had expanded onto the continent. Unlike Mark, Derek had no indecision about his midlife goals. Derek knew what he wanted. He wanted to go down in history.

The grand Maybach, a Mercedes-built limousine, was specially fitted with armor plate. Derek knew that if his secret plots were discovered his safety would be in jeopardy. His driver, Hans, had graduated from a special German course in tactical chauffeuring.

The leather-lined owner's compartment of the Maybach was fitted with highly polished conservative Germanic wood and a bevy of electronic devices. Hardin punched a button instantly connecting him to his London offices.

"I want the plane ready by noon. There's serious trouble in Tamar. I'm needed there." Derek was speaking to his trusted assistant, Robert Marsden. Marsden knew that oil had been discovered some years ago on the small Pacific island, ruled by a playboy King. Derek had never fully explained his involvement with Tamar, but had only rather vaguely told his aide that he was investing in the development of oil. Robert Marsden, 51, was an Oxford man who had been his eccentric superior's right hand man for 20 years. Hardin was a slim man who bought his shirts and suits on London's Jermyn Street. In more recent years Marsden had been allowed to make many important business decisions without consulting Derek.

Hardin's other long-time aide was Elizabeth Cannon. She was a licensed solicitor who, in recent years, had devoted full time to Derek's interests. She was educated in law at Oxford. Both Marsden and Cannon were paid one million pounds annually by Derek's corporation, Global Albion Ltd.

Over the years, Derek had found ways to assure himself of the absolute loyalty and secrecy of his two assistants, not the least of which was their inordinately large stipends and benefits.

Elizabeth Cannon was just past 40 with an incisively quick mind. She customarily wore short skirts and heels that were high by English business standards. Elizabeth was a very pretty short-haired blonde. Some in Global Albion's offices had speculated that there was an ongoing affair between Elizabeth and Derek, but there was no evidence to support the speculation, save Hardin's well-known fondness for pretty women.

The two assistants were the only ones to know of Hardin's investment in Tamar. What they did not know was that the dealings with Tamar's ruler were a clever cover for Derek's real interest—a daring and dangerous activity.

"Is there anything I should attend to before we go?" Derek asked Robert Marsden from the limousine.

"You'll remember you have the conference here at 10:00. Also Helinger, in Hamburg, needs to talk to you. And, too, Anteau needs to talk to you. Or, if you like, I can attend to him."

With his mind on Tamar, Derek had nearly forgotten the 10:00 o'clock conference. It was with a banker from Los Angeles. Derek had made a deal to buy the Los Angeles bank, but it had been blocked by the U.S. regulators. He suspected his old nemesis, Mark Stevens, was behind the refusal. The American banker was meeting with Derek to seek a damage settlement against Global Albion over the failure of the deal. Derek didn't intend to pay a single pence and, in fact, intended to demand damages of his own.

As was his habit, Derek abruptly terminated the call to Robert without saying goodbye.

As the big car entered the outskirts of London, Derek punched the button that immediately connected him to Gustav Helinger. Herr Helinger was the head of Global Albion's newly acquired bank—Derek's third in Germany.

Although German, Helinger spoke perfect English—a requirement of the German educational system. Hardin had placed a million euro limit on Helinger's power to make loans without the prior approval of Hardin or, in Derek's absence, Marsden's approval.

"Sir, we have a manufacturing customer who requires a loan of 25 million euros. I need your approval. We've never loaned him more than a million before."

"Send me his financial statements together with your summary of his credit worthiness," ordered Derek.

"To your car, sir?"

"Of course to the car. Do it at once. I'm nearing the City." Global Albion's offices were in London's financial district called "The City." Again, Derek abruptly terminated the call without another word.

Managing to avoid much of the congestion of the City by using side streets, the chauffeur pulled up to the side entrance of Derek's building, while he concluded his call to Anteau in Paris. Claude Anteau was the President of Derek's Paris bank.

"Yes, go ahead. I analyzed the papers over the weekend." Derek was giving his approval to acquiring a Lyon bank."

The uniformed doorman snapped open the limousine door. Without a word, Derek emerged from the Maybach. The doorman hurried ahead of Derek and opened the door to the building. Inside, another uniformed man held open the door of Derek's private lift.

"Good morning, sir."

Derek did not respond. As the lift ascended, the financial data from Hamburg arrived on his hand-held device.

Derek emerged from the lift into the reception room of his suite. As had been his custom since Oxford days, he was elegantly dressed in a dark, patterned Savile Row suit.

His dark hair had only a touch of gray and what wrinkles he had added to his strikingly dignified appearance.

Note pad in hand, an attractive female aide walked beside Derek as he strode from the lift to his private office. "Call our man in Hamburg. Tell him to go ahead with the loan and tell him his loan authority is now a full 25 million euros."

"Yes, Mr. Hardin," the young woman said as Derek abruptly closed the door to his office behind him.

The 10:00 o'clock meeting with the Los Angeles banker lasted less than 10 minutes. In his abrupt way, Derek had refused to pay any damages and had made his own threat to sue. The banker was quickly escorted to the lift by Derek's young aide.

Later, Derek's aides met in Elizabeth Cannon's office.

"I'm surprised," said Robert Marsden. "I thought Derek would make a compromise in the blink of an eye, if it was at all reasonable."

"I'm not surprised," answered Elizabeth.

"And why not? He agreed to the Lyon deal on no better terms."

"Because the banker is American, that's why. Surely you've noticed Mr. Hardin's attitude towards all things American."

"Yes, but business is business. That's why we're all in this hectic rat race." said Elizabeth.

"Not Derek Hardin. Not when it comes to America."

"Of course, I've seen it. Apparently the man despises America. Where does it all come from anyway?"

"I don't know. When I first came here, a senior P.A., called Katharine Smedley, perhaps you remember her, told me the story. When Hardin's parents were divorced, I think it was his father who took him to America. He must have got custody somehow from his mother. I suppose she had an affair or committed some unsavory act. Anyway, Katherine also said something about Derek's losing a court case trying to seize an American investment banking firm. Turned him totally sour on doing business in America," Robert explained.

"Yes, I heard something to that effect. From the story I heard, it was a company founded by an Oxford chum."

"More of an old Oxford enemy, from what Katharine told me," Robert added. "In fact she thought that the American investment firm had been founded by that same long-time enemy, a man called Mark Stevens."

"Not the Mark Stevens who is the American Secretary of Treasury? Or was until recently."

"The very same man."

"Well, we both know it's not wise to know too much about our Mr. Derek Hardin."

"Maybe it's the mystery about him that makes me want to stay with him. That and the power."

"More like that and the money." Robert hesitated. "We know the man's a complete neurotic. But I think we should not speak more of it."

"More than a neurotic, he's got a crazy streak. There's no explaining him anymore than explaining Adolph Hitler or any other tyrant. But I quite agree with you, ours is not to reason why, as long as he makes us rich." Robert smiled. "I like being rich."

Neither of Hardin's aides knew that it was Mark Stevens, who, as Secretary of Treasury, had blocked Hardin's acquisition of the San Francisco bank. That Hardin, in fact, had offered much more for the bank than he had admitted. And that the failure of the attempted acquisition had escalated the hatred Hardin had had for years toward America in general, and in particular, his Oxford enemy, Mark Stevens.

CHAPTER FIVE

"If I were you, I'd sure work in a trip to Rome."

As Mark's jet neared London's Heathrow, Rolf's words echoed in his mind.

Mark picked up the intercom. "Do we have enough fuel to make it to Rome?"

"Yes, sir. We have enough. Shall I change the flight plan?"

"Yes. We're going to Rome."

Mark remembered the time years ago when at Heathrow he had intended to board a plane to San Francisco, but had impulsively jumped on a flight to Rome. He'd had a sudden urge to see Christina. Really, to spy on her. To see if she really loved her wealthy new husband, Otello Bagliani. The older, but virile, mogul from whom she would come to inherit the newspaper, *Il Verita.*

Mark had not resisted the urge to see Christina then, and he decided not to resist her now.

His plane was over France when he reached Christina at her offices at *Il Verita.*

"I'm so glad you're coming," she said excitedly. "I have a meeting this afternoon. My two investigative reporters flew in from Indonesia yesterday. The situation looks even more dangerous than we thought."

"Can you hold the meeting until I get there? I'm over France right now."

"I'll send a car for you," said Christina. "No, wait, I'll come for you myself. I'll have supper brought in for the meeting."

Mark was grim-faced as he hung up the phone. Instead of a romantic interlude, it looked as if serious trouble were in the air.

Mark looked at Christina's blond hair flowing with the wind as her convertible raced toward Rome. It was the same red Ferrari Daytona she had driven 25 years ago, although now, with her wealth, she could have dozens of new Ferraris if she chose.

Forty years had fled by since the summer they had first made love—he a senior at Cal—she married to the inattentive older Antonio Movelli. Their furtive affair had precipitated her divorce. They each had been ultimately married to others. He to Priscilla, she to Otello Bagliani. Each of their spouses were now long dead. Although their busy lives were on separate continents, they met as often as they could. Mark had wondered if it were in part because of the physical distance that such strong feelings remained between them.

No matter how heavy the traffic Christina's foot did not ease off the accelerator. "The car has no power steering and is too hard to steer if I drive slow." Although her English was good, her native Italian showed in her speech more even than when she had lived in California.

"As if you needed an excuse to drive fast," Mark joked. "I can't imagine your driving anything except a Ferrari."

Despite the overhanging cloud of the impending meeting with the reporters, Mark was happier than he'd been in months. Christina's very presence was a tonic. In fact there was an excitement about the urgency of this evening's meeting—an excitement that he missed. My God, he had been more correct than he had realized when he had warned the President.

"We've located specifically where their training camp is—a little island near Borneo—Tamar." Christina had to speak loudly over the distinctive Ferrari whine of the engine, and the wind. "My people are working out a plan to infiltrate their organization—or at least try."

"This will make a banner story for *Il Verita*," Mark said.

"I'm still not certain where it will all lead. I don't want to tip them off by a story when the information really should go to the authorities. I'd want to stop whatever they're planning. Apparently they intend to blow up the American Embassy here in Rome. Maybe even your embassies in other countries too."

"God," said Mark disgustedly. "Knox has totally ignored our warnings—repeated warnings. The whole damned United States government is asleep. If your people can get some hard information, maybe I could wake them up. I don't know."

The meeting in Christina's office came quickly to the point. The two young reporters, Mario and Roberto, were unshaven because of their long trip from the small Pacific island. They had passed themselves off to the terrorists as exactly what they were—reporters for *Il Verita*. But they had pretended to be secret enemies of the United States. Months ago, on their first trip, they had convinced the leaders that they wanted to organize a plot to add Rome to the terrorists' list of U. S. embassies to be destroyed.

"Yes, they plan to destroy major U. S. embassies across the globe, all on the same day," Mario explained in Italian with Christina translating to Mark. "We're to be the leaders here in Rome."

"I'm sure they have some targets in the United States itself," Roberto added. He spoke enough English to talk directly to Mark. "But they're keeping their plans for each target totally separate. We're supposed to find people in Italy for training in Tamar. I'm sure they are doing the same thing in the other countries."

"Where are you supposed to get the money to do this?" Mark asked.

"They get it to us through a bank here," said Mario, again with Christina translating.

"We think it originates in England, but we're not sure," translated Christina.

"They're very secretive," said Roberto. "We haven't been able to find much about their methods."

"But my banking connections here in Rome think the money comes from London to Switzerland to Tamar," Christina explained to Mark.

"Are you sure they're plotting to bomb all these embassies?" Mark asked.

"Only here in Rome for sure," said Roberto. "But there's nothing so special about Rome."

"Why else would all those men from other countries be at the training camps?" Christina pointed out.

"Why else, indeed," said Mark. "They're up to something big."

The meeting lasted less than two hours. The two reporters were to return to Tamar after they spent a few days with their families.

The reporters were certain they were being carefully watched and knew they probably were being fed a certain amount of disinformation. They also knew if they were discovered it would mean their lives.

"Very brave young men," Mark said after Mario and Roberto had gone.

Christina nodded her assent.

"I'm going to call the President as soon as it's morning in Washington. But, frankly, I doubt that he'll pay much attention to me. He lives in a dream world."

"Not much different from the rest of world. Europe included," Christina responded. "But, I'd rather you call him from London. I don't want to have anyone figure out you got your latest information from *Il Verita*. Not if we can help it."

"All right. I'll call from London."

It was nearly midnight when they arrived at Christina's large Mediterranean villa in Rome's Parioli district. Together in bed in the ornate master suite, they continued talking about the meeting and the information *Il Verita's* journalists had reported.

Christina had expected that they would make love, but she could see that Mark was having difficulty staying awake as they talked. "You must be exhausted. It's been a long day," she said.

But Mark didn't answer. He had dozed off. Gently she pulled the blanket up around him. "We can make love in the morning," she whispered and gently kissed him on the cheek. She was so happy Mark was in Rome. She wondered if they'd ever be really together. Not just snatching a few days or hours here and there. At times like this she wanted more, but perhaps it simply was not meant to be. Soon, she too was asleep.

When Mark first awoke he didn't realize he was in Christina's bed. Then he reached for her, but she was not there. His hand touched a note left on her pillow:

Dear One,

Join me in the breakfast room. I'll be waiting.

Your Christina

Still a little groggy after his long sleep, Mark descended the grand staircase wearing the red robe Christina customarily left in the bathroom for him. The antique grandfather clock in the foyer told him it was 10:15.

Christina looked enticing, sitting over coffee. Her long blond hair tumbled down the back of her silken purple robe. She put down her copy of *Il Verita*.

"Good morning," she said, smiling. "You must have rested well. I'll ring for breakfast for you."

Mark kissed her on the cheek and sat opposite her. "What's the news this morning?" Mark asked, nodding at the newspaper she had put down on the glass breakfast table.

"The headline says: 'Lover falls asleep without making love,'" she laughed. "An American custom?"

"We'll see about that." Mark stood and slipped his hand inside the front of her robe.

She held his hand for a moment and then lifted it away. "First you have some breakfast and then I have a little surprise for you."

The servant brought Mark his coffee, butter and hard roll. "And just what is your surprise?" he laughed. "You Italian women always interest me with your little games."

"What do you mean. 'Italian women?' Just how many Italian women do you have anyway?"

"Hundreds. No thousands. They wear me out."

When Mark finished eating, he took her hand. "All right I'm well fed. Let's go back upstairs. I want to see your 'surprise,'" he said.

"No. Not upstairs. Come with me." She led him by the hand to the foyer and opened the front door of the villa.

There parked on the driveway in the bright sunlight was a long black Mercedes Benz car—its windows darkened. "Do you remember, my love?" she asked.

"Of course, I do. I'll never forget." Mark was flooded with the vivid memory of the time, years ago, when on the way to the Leonardo DeVinci airport, he had impulsively ordered the chauffeur to divert his chartered car to see Christina one last time before returning to San

Francisco. The driver had discretely left them alone while they desperately made love on the back seat of the car—each assuming it would be their last time together. Of course Mark would never forget that afternoon.

"I had the car brought around this morning, "Christina said. "It's my 'little surprise.'"

"You Italian women astound me," he chuckled, as he took her by the arm and pulled her toward the car. "At least this one does."

When they had finished, they slipped back into their robes and held each other. "It's been too long," she said. "It's different for you, you have all those other women."

"No, Christina, my dear. That's just it. You've spoiled me. There are no others."

That afternoon they lounged by Christina's elegant indoor Roman pool. Mark had just finished his telephone conversation with Rodney Ashley in London.

"How is Rodney?" Christina inquired. She knew Mark had known Rodney since their Oxford days, but she had never met him.

"He's all excited about this hotel venture. He wants to confer with me about it."

"It wouldn't be you if you weren't hurrying off to some meeting or another."

"Since I quit government, the Oxford Union has been wanting me to speak there. I may just take them up on it."

"Mark, my dear, I want you to think about something while you're in England."

"What?" For a quick moment he wondered if she was thinking of marriage, but he knew better. Christina would never leave her *Il Verita* and both knew he had his life in America.

"Is that panic I see on your face?" she laughed, pointing at him. "You didn't think I was going to suggest marriage, did you?"

That was Christina for you, he thought. Ever insightful. Ever direct.

Mark laughed in return.

"No, my dear it's not marriage," she continued. "For months now you've been complaining about your President's policies. And how you say he's blind to this terrorist threat."

"That's why I resigned. What more can I do?"

"You could run for President yourself. That's what you could do." There was conviction in her voice.

Mark paused for a moment. "Christina, you flatter me. But you don't understand about American politics. Knox and I are both Republicans. There's no way I could get the Republican nomination away from a sitting President. Even Ronald Reagan couldn't do that from Gerald Ford. And even if I could, it would ruin the chances of the party. The Democrats are sure to nominate a strong candidate."

"Well, I think you should at least think about it."

They made love again that night. Coupled with their passion, there was always a sort of melancholy in not knowing when they would again be together.

The next morning they said goodbye in the driveway. Christina's chauffeur was to drive Mark to his plane— in the same black Mercedes. "It won't be the same car without you," Mark said. "Could you get away for a few days in London?"

"We'll see. I'll try. But I'm serious. I think you should think about running for President. I know you, my dear restless friend. I think it's something you have to do."

As his plane crossed the channel and England came into view, it was not a run for the Presidency that Mark thought about. What was on his mind was how much Christina meant to him. He recalled how he had returned to his Oxford studies after their weekend in Paris. The tempestuous weekend when Christina had told him she planned to marry Otello. As angry as he had been, he knew then that he could never forget her. And now, as England came into view below, he knew more than ever that Christina was in his blood.

CHAPTER SIX

"Mr. Secretary, the President will speak to you in one minute. He's just finishing his call." It was President Knox's secretary. Mark was calling from his London town house.

"And how have you been, Sherri?" Mark chatted as he waited. "Just fine, sir. But things aren't the same since you left. Only yesterday . . . the President is ready, Mr. Stevens."

"Mark, how the hell are you?" Knox spoke as if they remained the best of friends. It had been four months since Mark had resigned.

"I'm fine Stuart. Miss the action a bit, but—"

"I envy you, Mark. Yeah, I'd miss the action too. But it must be great to be rid of the pressure."

"You must have a lot less pressure with me off your back," Mark joked, albeit rather feebly.

Mark pictured the last time he was in the oval office. It was true that he missed the action of being close to power, but he didn't miss at all having no real influence on that power.

The President laughed. "You sound relaxed. That's great. As I say I envy you."

Mark knew this was mostly bull, but that was Knox's way. That trait had been a big factor in getting him to the White House.

"Stuart, it's fun chatting like this, but—"

"Like the old days, isn't it?"

"Yes, but I called for a reason."

"I'm sure you did. What is it?"

"I've learned more about this terrorist business."

"Oh, that."

"Look, Stuart. I've got specific provable information about a plot to bomb the U.S. Embassy in Rome."

"Come on, Mark, we get warnings like that all the time."

"Stuart, I'm dead serious. And so are these men. I know where their base is and who some of them are. What's more—"

"Mark. I'm sorry but I've got to take this other call. I appreciate your telephoning. I'm sure you wouldn't have unless you thought—"

"Stuart, it's not just what I thought. I've got real evidence. Credible evidence."

"All right, Mark, I'll have someone at the CIA look into it. I'll tell them to call you."

"Okay, Stuart. I guess I've done all I can. I know we've disagreed about this before, but I beg you. You've got to take this seriously."

"I will take it seriously. I'll have Harry notify the CIA. But you've got to remember, it's been years since any terrorist attacks. What more can I do? I've got a million things on my plate."

"I know. I know. But why do I get the feeling that nothing is really going to happen?"

"Dammit Mark. This sort of thing belongs in the Homeland Securities' lap. They've told me before they know of no plots. But Harry will notify them. Now, I've got to take this call. Good to talk to you, Mark."

That fraud, Mark thought to himself. I'm not going to hold my breath waiting for any calls from the CIA.

"What do you intend to do, Mr. President?" Harry Manning asked. The Chief of Staff had been sitting in the oval office throughout the conversation.

"Nothing, Harry. Absolutely nothing. Stevens is an alarmist. Always has been. We've no cause to worry about terrorist threats. That was a long time ago. It was a mistake to offer him Treasury."

Knox lit a forbidden cigarette and took a deep drag. "Well, hell, on second thought," he went on. "Maybe you'd better notify Homeland Security and the CIA. You know what I think, Harry?"

"No, sir. What?"

"I'm thinking there's a possibility Stevens may be trying to set me up for a campaign issue. I think he may make a try to get the nomination from me in the primaries. You know. Creating an issue."

"Oh, I wouldn't worry about that. He wouldn't have a chance."

Manning had been with Knox since he was a Congressman. Although he knew his boss to be a shrewd politician, he also knew the man had a streak of the paranoid.

The President held up his hand before Manning could continue. "I know what you're thinking, Harry. You think I see political threats under every rock."

"Oh, no sir," Manning lied.

"Harry, make the calls! I don't want to be giving Stevens any campaign fodder."

Manning knew he would make the calls, but he wasn't going to push anybody. Hell, the agencies were on top of things. And as the President had just said, it had been years since the terrorists had been silenced.

Mark was in the rear passenger seat of his vintage London Rolls-Royce Phantom limousine. Jorge was driving across London from Mark's Belgravia townhouse to the Garrick Club in West End's theater district where he was to dine with Rodney Ashley. Rodney and Mark had been close friends since their Oxford days. Upon Rodney's graduation, his father, Lord Stanley Ashley, had entrusted his son with a share of the family wealth with an admonition: "Invest it wisely, invest it conservatively." But Rodney had overextended himself. After Mark came to his friend's rescue with an infusion of cash, they had formed the Worcester Fund, named after their Oxford college. The fund with Rodney as managing director was now a large owner of real estate in the United Kingdom.

As the limousine made its way along Piccadilly, Mark felt the same excitement he had first felt when Rodney and he had driven the famed street in their taxi crammed with luggage. It had been Mark's first time in London. Mark recalled how dazzled he had been when they had driven near Buckingham Palace and had passed Queen Elizabeth and Prince Philip in their royal limousine. Ever since, London had been exciting to Mark.

The car made its way through the busy Leicester Square to the Garrick Club. For more than 150 years the private club had been a refuge for famous actors and celebrities. The elegant building and its beautiful rooms spoke silently of long tradition.

"Good evening, Mr. Stevens. A bit nasty out there." The elderly attendant had served many famous persons and was part of the Garrick Club's tradition. He took Mark's coat.

"Thank you, Robert." Mark had not visited the club in over a year, but he would never forget Robert. The white-haired, bushy mustached man looked to be straight out of a Charles Dickens novel.

"Mr. Stevens, sir, you have a message at the desk."

Mark,

Will be an hour late to Garrick. Have a Rob Roy on me. Anxious to tell you about hotel deal. It's the largest transaction of my life. Need your input and approval.

Rodney

Mark chose to sit at one of the several side tables in the main dining room, where he and Rodney could talk undisturbed. The long center table that dominated the room was traditional for members to hold collegial conversation. But tonight it had only half a dozen members and Mark did not recognize any of them.

"A Rob Roy, sir?" the female server asked. Mark had not seen her before, but she had evidently been told of Mark's regular drink. A mixture of Scotch whiskey with a bit of sweet vermouth.

"Yes, please. Thank you. What is your name?"

"Cecily, sir." She was an attractive woman about 30. Women employees in the London clubs, traditionally male bastions, were common now, although the club still followed the distinctly British tradition of expecting women guests to leave the long center table to men.

"Thank you, Cecily, It will be a while until Lord Ashley arrives for dinner."

"Yes, sir."

Jolly male laughter arose from the center table. Evidently someone had told a joke. Mark loved the dry English sense of humor.

As Mark sipped his Rob Roy, his thoughts drifted to his relationship with Rodney and his family. The corpulent son of a Lord had had the room opposite Mark's at Worcester. At first Mark had been intimidated by the thought of Rodney's one day being a Lord by inheritance, but he had soon learned that under Rodney's stuffy veneer, as with many Englishmen, lay a warm and friendly human being. After several weeks into the term, Rodney had invited Mark to London's Chelsea to meet his father, the venerable Sir Sidney Ashley, member of the House of Lords, and his beautiful wife, the Lady Mavis Ashley.

Mark finished his Rob Roy and ordered another.

He remembered well the painting of Castle Enfield that hung in the entry hall of the Ashley home. Castle Enfield was Lady Ashley's ancestral home in England's Cotswolds. Rodney had invited the inexperienced Mark for Christmas at the massive stately country home. Lady Ashley had introduced Mark to English high society. Mark had been awestruck with the way they took their great wealth and status for granted.

Mark looked at his watch. He hoped Rodney would not be much longer. He decided to nurse his drink rather than have still another. The men at the center table were dining now and their conversation was intermittent.

"There you are!" bellowed a voice from the dining room door, causing the diners to look up. Mark stood at the sound his friend's voice and was soon in the grasp of the ever overweight Rodney. "Ever so sorry to keep you waiting, but my meeting in Southampton took much too long."

Rodney was bubbling with enthusiasm. "Frankly, I'm not certain if we should raze the old beast of a hotel and build something spectacular, or remodel. We'll have to do a cost analysis."

As they ordered and ate their dinner. Rodney enthusiastically talked on and on about the hotel deal. "Forty-five million pounds.

The grounds alone are easily worth that and much more. It's been in their family for generations and they don't realize its value. They only know their income stream has dropped off."

Mark smiled inwardly. He supposed the hotel deal was interesting, but the real pleasure was in seeing Rodney's excitement. What a change from an overweight purposeless son of a rich lord, contented with ordinary grades at Oxford, a "gentleman's third," to becoming one of the most respected business leaders in the U. K. The last report showed the Worcester Fund to be worth in excess of nine billion pounds.

Rodney reminded Mark of the way he had been years ago—when he had nervously quit a highly paid position in San Francisco to start his own firm. What enthusiasm Mark had had for business and financial success. But he had learned something important about himself. He could not live by material success alone. It was not enough. In one way Mark envied Rodney and his enthusiasm for business. Those were happy days in Mark's life. He wished he could share Rodney's enthusiasm, but it was clear that he had to seek his satisfaction outside of business. That was why he had accepted Stuart Knox's offer to be Secretary of the Treasury. The excitement of business was in his past.

Dinner was over. They retired to another room to have their port. "You must come to the country with Rebecca and me this weekend. The children may come. Depends on the weekend activities of the grandchildren."

Rodney, a grandfather, Mark thought. If Pris had not been killed, perhaps he, too, would have grandchildren. Mark wondered if that would have ever been enough for his own restless spirit. He would never know.

"I'm sorry, my friend. I haven't seen Rebecca and the children in lord knows how long. But Monday I'm to speak to the Oxford Union. Worcester's new Provost has invited me to High Table for Sunday night. Why don't you come with me? I'm certain it would be all right. Have you met the new Provost, Nigel Peterson?"

"Yes, I met him here in London once—a fund raiser. I'd love to join you, but the family weekend . . ." said Rodney.

"You could drive over to Oxford Sunday afternoon. I'm sure it would be all right with Peterson. It'll give us a chance to reminisce. You know very well it will be okay with Rebecca."

"I'll do it!" said Rodney. "It will be like our university days once again."

CHAPTER SEVEN

After its final refueling stop in Singapore, Derek's jet had landed at the Tamar airport. The runway had been lengthened to better accommodate Derek's plane and to handle missile-launching warplanes. Delivery of the planes, being secretly bought from China, was expected shortly.

The limousine, flags flying from each front fender, did not take Hardin to his hotel, but instead drove him directly to the adjacent military headquarters of General Assad. Assad was the person who actually ran the country—not the free-spending King who lived most of his time in Switzerland and New York.

General Assad's stark headquarters building was in the interior of the semi-tropical island near the training grounds. These were facilities that had been financed by Derek Hardin and had nothing to do with the development of oil on the island.

Assad met Derek as he alighted from the limousine outside the small single story office building. The general was dressed simply in a combat uniform with no ribbons and with no insignia of his rank. His face was clean-shaven except for a bushy mustache that had nearly turned white in contrast to his thick black hair. He had an upright military bearing.

Despite his long flight, Derek was dressed in one of his elegant Savile Row suits. Without waiting for the General to speak, Derek spoke sharply to Assad: "Well, what is it that is so cursed important that you couldn't tell me by secure line and that I have to fly all the way from London to hear? It had better be important."

"Of course it's an important matter. Otherwise I would not be spending my time on it." Assad spoke perfect English, having been sent by his Saudi Arabian father to be educated at Eton and then Cambridge. Derek knew that the General was one of the few people in his life that would not be backed off by his overbearing attitude. That was why Derek respected him, as much as Derek could ever respect anyone. And that was why Hardin had entrusted Assad with many millions of pounds to carry out their secret mission to destroy exactly ten targeted embassies of the United States of America in various countries. Assad had been an al Qaeda member and a young assistant to bin Laden. After bin Laden's death, he had made his way to power in Tamar.

"Come into my office and I'll brief you. There have been serious new developments."

General Assad's stark headquarters building was in the interior of the semi-tropical island near the training grounds.

Assad ushered Derek into his private office, where they were alone. The office was sparsely furnished with a simple desk with two well-worn tan leather side chairs. On the wall behind the General was a dusty framed photograph of Osama bin Laden. At one side of the desk was a table laden with modern communication equipment. Otherwise the office looked like a Second World War headquarters.

Without waiting for the General, Derek sat in one of the side chairs.

As Assad sat behind the desk, Derek spoke: "Well, what is it that is so cursed important?"

Assad was unfazed by Hardin's rudeness. "As I told you, of course it's important."

"Get on with it then."

"We have spies in our midst!"

"Spies?"

"They're connected in some way with an Italian newspaper. They've been in training by us to bomb the American embassy in Rome. But our suspicions were aroused when we learned they flew to Rome on an excuse and then flew back only two days ago."

"What are they up to? Are they connected to the Italian government?"

"We had them followed in Rome. They met with the publisher of the newspaper, *Il Verita,* it's called."

"I see."

"But most important, and that's why I asked you to come here at once…"

"Damn it, get on with it," Derek again interrupted impatiently.

Assad frowned at Derek's insolence. "Also in the meeting in Rome was a former United States high official. Mark Stevens is his name."

"Mark Stevens!" Derek's voice rose to a near shout.

"You know him?"

"Yes, I know him." Hardin's expression was grim. "Unfortunately I know Mr. Mark Stevens very well."

"I'm told this Stevens has been warning the American parliament of an attack. We think his information has been coming from these spies and that Italian newspaper."

"Kill them! Kill them at once. No, wait. Eliminate them tomorrow after I leave for London." commanded Derek.

"As you say. It will be done."

"And make certain their employer knows they are dead." Grimly, Derek paused. "Remember next time something like this comes up, there is no need to ask me to fly half way around the world."

The next morning, before Derek boarded his plane, he held a brief conversation on the tarmac with Assad. "I'm not completely satisfied with the idea of blowing up the embassies. We must plan the next step."

"The next step?"

"Yes. I want something spectacular. Something that will make September 11, 2001 seem like a minor incident."

"Do you have anything in mind?"

"No, but I will. You'll see. I will. The embassy plan is only a beginning. In fact I may cancel the embassy idea when I decide on something else."

At the airstrip Assad and his aide watched Derek's plane fade into the distant sky. "What drives a man like that?" asked the aide.

"I don't expect you to understand. It's the same devil that drove bin Laden. I know that devil well. You see, it's what drives me."

CHAPTER EIGHT

It was a friendly group of intellectuals who walked down
the narrow passageway to Worcester College's Old Bursary
for the traditional Sunday night ritual. Present were some
dozen persons including Mark and Rodney. Three were
women. All the males were dressed in formal, mostly
rumpled, jackets and dark trousers—what Americans
called tuxedos, a term not used in Britain. Graying hair
was abundant. One of the women, an Oxford graduate,
was a Justice of the Australian Supreme Court. She was
in England researching for a book. The Justice exhibited
a good sense of humor, making wisecracks and laughing
at those of others. The other women were from other
Oxford colleges. One specialized in comparative religion
at Exeter College. The third, called Fenilla Collins, was
from Christ Church, the largest of Oxford's nearly 40
colleges. She was considerably younger than the other
two—40 or younger. From their brief conversation, Mark
picked up that she was knowledgeable in world affairs.
He didn't learn whether she was a tutor or held some
other position at Christ Church. Mark saw that the other
two women were dressed conservatively, even drably.
However, in contrast, Fenilla Collins wore a brightly

colored yellow blouse over her long stylish black skirt. She had attractive long red hair. She was an engaging and bright young woman. Mark wanted to talk to her more before the evening was over—his attraction toward Fenilla reminded him of his feelings toward Christina in their earlier years.

The participants served themselves hors d'oeuvres as they chatted. The room was smallish and extremely old. Tradition hung from the very walls—walls that were covered with paintings that appeared nearly as old as the building itself. The guests, together with the several small serving tables and the stuffed chairs, totally filled the room that buzzed with various conversations. Mark guessed that they all knew he was the newly resigned American Secretary of Treasury, but his status did not seem to impress them, as it would have at an American college.

Mark half expected to see the new British Prime Minister, as he knew she was an Oxford graduate. But she was not present.

Mark was thoroughly enjoying the conversations. The content was distinctly Oxford—much more intellectual than it would be in America. Some of the men were tutors at Worcester and a few were from other Oxford colleges. Some held government posts in addition to their teaching duties. One tall fellow was the President of the U. K. subsidiary of a Chinese bank. Another, the youngest of the lot, was an executive with Bentley Motor cars at Crewe in the North of England. Bentley had been owned by Volkswagen for a number of years now. Mark assumed the man was German, although he spoke English with neither an English, nor a German accent.

The atmosphere stimulated Mark. Years ago it had been hinted by the then-Provost that a teaching position might be offered, if he desired. Mark had been discrete in declining the suggestion, but he could see why many were attracted to the sophisticated scholarly environment. It would have been an interesting life, but for Mark, not enough action.

Nigel Peterson, Worcester's Provost, announced: "Everyone, its time to go to Hall. Supper awaits." Animatedly each in the group donned the academic gowns that were customarily worn by all at dinner.

They all marched along the cloisters of the old building into the high ceilinged Dining Hall. It being Sunday, the number of students was somewhat reduced. All respectfully stood as the procession of academics and guests filed down the aisle to the High Table at the far end of the Hall. The table was on a platform above the main floor. The 12 took their places around the grand table with the Provost standing in the commanding position facing toward the students. Peterson said the customary Latin prayer. The many dozens of chairs noisily scraped the wooden floor as the diners seated themselves.

Happily, Mark was seated next to Fenilla Collins. He wondered if Peterson had so arranged it, noticing Mark's attraction to the young woman and their mutual interest in world affairs.

"Are you a tutor at Christ Church?" Mark inquired as they began their first course. He had to speak loudly to be heard over the din of the many conversations taking place in the large room with its high ceilings.

"No, actually I'm working on a special project. I have a grant, you see. I specialize in Malaysia—actually the entire southwest Pacific."

Mark was fascinated; he wondered whether she knew of the terrorist threat brewing on Tamar. He would skirt around the subject for now. "Are you from London?" he asked.

"In actual fact, I was born in Ireland, but when my father died my mother brought me to London. I was too young to remember Ireland."

"Maybe Ireland explains your red hair."

"Probably does," she responded with a delightful laugh.

Mark noticed her attractive complexion, untouched by the sun. The dishes were removed and the second course was served as they continued their small talk.

"In actual fact, Secretary Stevens—" she began.

"Call me Mark. I insist you call me Mark," he said. "You were about to say?"

"I was about to say," she paused briefly. "Mark. I asked the Provost to seat me next to you."

"Oh, really."

"Yes, you see. I read in our press about your exchange with your Congress."

"You did? Over here? You mean about my talk with Congressman Raymond about this new terrorist organization?"

"Yes, I believe that was the name of the Congressman. From what was reported in the U.K. press you felt there was a serious terrorist threat. In fact there has been some speculation, at least amongst the people I talk to, that your warnings to President Knox led to your resignation."

"I really ought not to comment on my reasons for resignation."

"No. No. I completely understand." She smiled. "I wasn't pressing you on that point. You see, the reason I was eager to talk with you tonight is that my work shows that your source, I'm assuming it's *Il Verita*, is accurate. You see, I spent several days on Tamar last summer. The authorities saw to it that I didn't stay any longer, but I saw enough to know that there are foreigners—known troublemakers left over from the old days—all over the island. I saw them in the few hotels and restaurants they have there. They disappear into the interior during the day. I'm quite certain, although I can't prove it, that they are being updated in terrorist tactics. The older ones teaching the younger ones. Worse yet, I suspect much of the money is coming from the U.K.—although it's just my suspicion at this point."

Mark was astounded. Here, in what was an academic setting and what he had expected would be a mundane conversation about world affairs, he had found verification of what Christina's reporters had told him.

"Have you informed anyone in your government of your findings?" Mark asked her.

"Indeed I have. At least at the lower levels. I'm uncertain how high up the information has gone, if at all. Regretfully our government is often slow to react. It's sort of a tradition with us," she smiled. "If you couldn't get the attention of your President, what chance do I have?"

Mark nodded his agreement. "What do you intend to do about it?"

"I'm doing it right now," Fenilla said. She had a smile on her face.

"I'm sorry. You're doing it right now?"

"Yes, you see, I'm having a conversation with an important American voice—you. We British aren't about to do anything on our own. America is the leader of the world. The only leader as far as I can see." She paused for a few seconds appearing reluctant to go on. "I'm not certain I should admit this, but when I heard you were to speak to the Oxford Union tomorrow, I had planned to attend. I wasn't originally invited to this do at Worcester tonight. But when I learned you were to be here, I saw to it that I was invited."

"You flatter me. But I've done all I can. I have no power. You're right, that's why I resigned. Knox simply won't pay serious attention. As a matter of fact I telephoned him only the other day."

"I'm not flattering you at all. I don't know if you realize the respect you have in the U.K. and, I'm sure, in America as well," she was talking quickly, confidently. "I'll come right to the point. Have you considered running for your Presidency?"

Mark was both flabbergasted and amused. "My dear young woman, you may be an expert in certain areas, but I'm not sure you know America. To answer your question. Yes, I have considered seeking the Presidency. But only quite perfunctorily. A third party candidate in America doesn't have a chance. Ross Perot became a laughing stock. And running against a sitting President of your own party? Not a chance. One of the most attractive third party candidates in American history, Theodore Roosevelt, was soundly defeated. All he accomplished was to throw the election to the opposite party. And

Roosevelt had already been President before, for God's sake."

"But remember, Mark, Theodore Roosevelt and his Bull Moose Party didn't have the issue you would have—terrorism. He was really running as much for his own ego as on any issue. And you're forgetting one thing."

Mark was taken aback. "And what, pray, is this one thing you seem so certain about?"

"Abraham Lincoln. He was elected in a three party race. But he had the important issues of his time. Slavery and the Union. And he won."

Mark sat stunned. He had stopped eating while Fenilla was talking—staring at her. How on Earth did this youthful Englishwoman have such a comprehensive understanding of American history?

"And another thing," she continued. "Even if you didn't win, as you think would be the case, you would wake up the world. You would make it your major campaign issue. They would have to listen to you. The entire world would pay attention."

"My, you do have a cause don't you. I must admit I admire your tenacity. You seem to have an answer for everything."

"I guess it's the Irish in me," she laughed again. Her delightful laugh.

When the meal was finished the students stood aside while those at High Table marched out of the Hall along the Cloisters to Old Bursary, where they removed their gowns. They ended the evening over port, chocolate and other tidbits in the Upper Senior Common Room, a beautifully paneled room dominated by a fireplace and still more historic paintings. Mark could not concentrate.

His mind kept returning to Fenilla Collins who had not joined the others for this final gathering. He could not get over her extensive knowledge of American history, let alone that she was aware of the Tamar situation. Mark hadn't remembered that Abraham Lincoln was elected in a three party race. His thoughts kept returning to possibly making his own run at the Presidency. This was the third person whose opinion he respected who had suggested he give it a try. Rolf, Christina, and now this Englishwoman. The most telling reason to undertake what he knew would be an exhausting ordeal had been raised by Fenilla. Even if he didn't stand a realistic chance of winning, he could awaken the nation and the world to the new terrorist threat.

CHAPTER NINE

After the evening's events at Worcester, Rodney and Mark met for a lager beer in the Nag's Head, a pub they frequented as college friends. Rodney had just driven to Oxford from Castle Enfield, his family country home in the Cotswolds.

"Look, Rodney, you do whatever you think best. The hotel deal is okay with me." The Nag's Head was nearly deserted on this late Sunday night. It was the same pub where Mark had lost his temper and had struck the obnoxious Derek Hardin the night of the Kennedy assassination. Derek's derogatory words about the fallen President were still fresh in Mark's mind. "Kennedy was no martyr. He was on a damnable political fund raising trip." Mark had angrily knocked Derek to the floor of the pub. Hardin's irrational hatred of all things American, and Mark's reaction that night were only the beginning of several confrontations between the two while Mark was at Oxford. Indeed, confrontations that had continued for years, even to the present day.

"You don't think I'm overextending the company again, do you?" Rodney asked, sipping his beer, unaware of Mark's thoughts about Derek.

Mark reached across the small table to put his hand on his friend's shoulder. "No, I don't. I have complete confidence in your ability." Mark drank some of his beer and continued. "Rodney, I have a confession to make. When I left Washington, I thought I would get involved in business again. But the problem, old friend, is that I just have no enthusiasm for business anymore."

"My God, man, I never thought I'd hear those words from your mouth. What would you ever do with yourself? I can't see you sitting in a rocking chair for the balance of your days."

"I don't know what I want. I really don't know. Some of my friends have been talking about my running for President, but that seems impossible."

"You as President! I say, old friend, Mark Stevens, President of the United States."

"Does the idea seem preposterous to you, too?"

"No, not preposterous. Just amazing. Do you think you'd stand a chance in politics?"

"Probably not, but it may be something I'll have to do."

"Have to do?"

The two friends, who had withheld little from one another for 40 years, talked for nearly two hours, nursing their beer. Mark explained the warnings that President Knox had ignored. He told of the meeting in *Il Verita's* offices with Christina and her reporters. He repeated the evening's conversations with Fenilla Collins. Rodney listened attentively, but said little except to ask the occasional question.

"You seem very concerned about this terrorism business."

"I am, but what can I do about it? I've done everything I can think of within the government, where the power is."

"You know," said Rodney. "My father was a great one for the word 'duty.'"

Mark knew that Rodney's father had been a decorated volunteer officer in the Great War and an illustrious member of Britain's House of Lords. "My father would have said you have a duty to alert the American people to this new threat. We've all gone to sleep in recent years. My father knew Winston Churchill in those early years. You know Churchill tried to warn Britain of the Hitler danger. From what you're telling me, someone needs to wake up America—indeed the world—before it's too late. I think perhaps this Collins woman is correct. It appears as if you're the one who can do it."

"But how?" Mark mumbled half to himself.

"There's one sure way. You can make a run for the Presidency. They'd have to listen to you then."

Both were somber as they parted. Rodney planned to drive back to the Cotswolds to be with his family and to use the telephone there to work on the hotel deal. Mark was staying at the Provost's Lodgings, where the third story guest room was his for the night. He planned a final touch-up of his remarks for his Oxford Union address that was to be the day after tomorrow.

For over an hour after he had gone to bed Mark had been unable to sleep. Had his friends been correct? Clearly a new September 11, 2001 was being planned by this new breed of terrorists. Had Fenilla Collins been correct? Christina would say so.

Was Rodney correct? Perhaps he did owe a duty to warn the nation, by making it a campaign issue.

His appearance before the Oxford Union was on his mind.

The ideas he had planned for his speech no longer seemed so important. Here at Oxford he had first espoused the new monetary system that had found its way into policy. In his speech he had planned to expound on his disagreement with the current high interest rate policy of the U. S. Federal Reserve and that of the European Central Bank, but that no longer seemed so important.

He gave up trying to sleep, and rose to dress. Nervously, he walked the familiar grounds of Worcester College, thinking. Should he warn of the threat? Or had he done enough? In the darkness he found a bench by the pond where he had done so much of his thinking as a student. He remembered how he used to talk to the ducks when he was seeking a solution to a problem. Tonight the ducks were quiet as he sat silently on the bench, pondering.

He found himself walking along the nearby New Hall Inn Street and onto St. Michael's Street. He entered the grounds of the Union and walked up the narrow path to the Debating Hall. Many great issues of the times had been debated in the tradition-filled hall.

What greater issue could there be today than the threat of more terrorist attacks upon an unprepared world? His decision became clear. He would scrap his intended remarks and go public with his concern. Perhaps he could finally make the Knox administration take serious action. Should he actually seek the Presidency? Maybe in the end he would have little choice.

CHAPTER TEN

Mark spent the day before his Oxford Union speech nostalgically walking the Oxford streets so familiar to him as a student. As he walked, he began formulating the wording of his address. An Oxford adage said that one did not really know his own opinion until he put it into specific words. He walked down busy High Street to The Examination Schools, where he had tested so well that he had won a "First," the highest honor for a graduating senior. He searched for words that would convey the seriousness of the terrorist threat. Still pondering his speech, he next entered the Clarendon Building and stood outside the room where, as a student about to graduate, he had faced an inquisition by the University on the false charges of plagiarism. It was only much later that Mark learned that the phony evidence had been contrived by the revenge-seeking Derek Hardin. A sense of self-assuredness came over Mark as he pictured himself delivering a convincing speech to the always-skeptical Oxford Union crowd.

Rodney's admonition about Winston Churchill came to mind. The great statesman's early warning about Nazi Germany had gone unheeded. Mark knew that he had a responsibility to awaken the sleeping world that was oblivious to this new threat. More than that, if this new generation would not listen, he must do something more. He would be compelled to make speech after speech, especially in the United States—to go before Congressional committees—to appear on television— even to buy TV time if he must. He must do everything possible. The speech would likely be only a beginning of his mission.

It was the next day, the day of his address. Mark wore a dark suit as he began the short walk from Worcester College to the Debating Hall. He was nervous. He was worried that his speech might not accomplish what he wanted.

He turned at the sound of running footsteps behind him. It was Rodney, breathlessly catching up to him.

"Rodney, what are you doing here? I expected you'd be in London working on the hotel deal."

"I couldn't stay away. This will be the most important speech of your life. I wanted to show my support. What you're doing is far more important than any hotel acquisition."

They walked side by side down Beaumont Street, the always-overweight Rodney catching his breath. "I appreciate your being here old friend. I only hope I can deliver. I must admit, I'm somewhat nervous," said Mark.

"I don't blame you. Your appearance here has been in the London newspapers. Your disagreement with Knox has made the newspapers here in England. The press is speculating you are going to make a major foreign policy speech. Perhaps even announce a run for the Presidency."

"I suppose I might be asked that question tonight."

"And your answer?"

"That I won't—run, that is." Mark paused, thinking. "Frankly Rodney I don't think I'd have a chance to get the Republican nomination away from Knox. For God's sake, he's the sitting President! You've got to understand the American political reality."

"But on the other hand?" questioned Rodney.

"As we were saying the other day, maybe it would be the only way I could arouse the nation. By making it a campaign issue." Mark paused as they walked, thinking.

"No, I'm not going to run. No way."

Three hours earlier Derek Hardin's jet had landed at London's Stansted airport. His driver had pulled the imposing black Maybach onto the tarmac and held the door open to Derek as he alighted from the plane.

"Welcome back, sir. Here are the morning newspapers." The chauffeur handed Hardin the London papers. Not saying a word, Derek sat in the rear seat of the mighty automobile and began scanning the papers. As the car made its way toward the City, an item on the third page of the *Daily Telegraph* startled Derek.

> *"Former U.S. Secretary of Treasury to address Oxford Union. Mr. Mark Stevens, who recently resigned as United States Secretary of the Treasury in a dispute with President Knox, will address the Oxford Union tonight. Speculation has it that Stevens will address the issue that reportedly led to his resignation. Stevens testified before*

*the U.S. Congress that the U.S. was facing
a serious and imminent terrorist threat."*

Derek lowered the chauffeur's window. "Take me to Oxford at once," he barked.

As Mark and Rodney approached the Oxford Union's Debating Hall on St. Michael's Street, the black Maybach pulled to a stop ahead of them. They saw the chauffeur open the passenger door.

"I wonder who that is?" asked Rodney.

Derek alighted from the car some 50 yards ahead.

"My God! Look!" Mark nearly shouted.

"No, it can't be! It's Derek. Derek Hardin," Rodney exclaimed.

"What in the hell is he doing here?" Mark asked.

"I'll wager he's read about your speech in the newspaper. I told you, you've gotten some publicity."

"Yes, but what possible interest would Derek Hardin have in a speech about terrorism?"

The Oxford Union's Debating Hall was arranged somewhat like the seating in Parliament. Mark and the Master, who was garbed in an academic gown and who was to introduce Mark, sat at the raised platform at the head of the large hall with several rows of cushioned pew-like seating on the right and left, facing each other. At the end of the hall, facing Mark, were a number of additional rows of seating. Stained glass windows interrupted the walls. Marble busts of various Oxford personages were arranged at the edges of the room. Dark faded portraits of long-dead persons hung on the walls. The room reeked of tradition and history and was filled to capacity, with some students standing along the walls.

As the Master droned on about Mark's qualifications Mark spotted Derek Hardin seated far to the rear. What is Derek up to now? Mark asked himself. Knowing Derek, the man was up to no good.

"And so, I present to you Mr. Mark Stevens," the Master concluded. "who, as a student reading economics at Oxford's own Worcester College, germinated the ideas that ultimately resulted in creation of our present day system of international monetary exchange, and until his recent resignation, was America's Secretary of the Treasury."

Mark stepped down from the podium to the historic table that served as the lectern. As had become his custom when addressing a large crowd, Mark looked around the hall appearing to look at each listener individually. He guessed that the group consisted of perhaps 250. About a third were dressed in academic gowns as had been required on most occasions when Mark was an Oxford student. His nervousness had stopped, replaced by a strong sense of purpose.

The Oxford Union had a long-standing reputation of being irreverent in its treatment of guest speakers, but no matter to Mark as he looked over the audience. He felt as if he were in charge. While most were of student age, some were older. He assumed they were faculty and perhaps some were from the press. As he began, he locked eyes with Derek Hardin. What was Derek doing here? he again asked himself.

Mark began: "Ladies and gentlemen, it is special to return to Oxford once more. And I emphasize the presence of ladies, because when I was a student here, there were no ladies in the Oxford Union." Mark paused long enough for the audience to chuckle at his reference to Oxford's former male only tradition. "Except of course for those who were students at Somerville College." Many in the audience laughed, apparently recalling that Somerville was an all female college in Mark's student days. "I say today, as I said then, 'Thank God for Somerville College, for my time at Oxford would have been bleak indeed without Somerville.'" This time most of the audience laughed. Mark felt he had established a kinship with the group.

He then launched into the meat of his message. He wanted to be short and to the point—to have an impact. He dramatically walked in front of the desk, turning first to his right. "Ladies and Gentlemen of Oxford, this great and influential university, I have come here to warn you." Mark paused, taking a few steps. "My country and yours, indeed the entire world, faces a renewed threat of terrorism that, if carried out will make the past look like only the beginning. I am here to tell you that our two nations have fallen asleep to this threat as we were asleep before the eleventh of September, 2001." The audience was quiet, attentive, some leaning forward.

Mark turned to his left. "I know that we spent a great deal of money after eleven, nine, naught one." He deliberately said the day of the month before the number of the month in the English tradition. "We spent the lives of many of our young men and women. Much of that money could have been used for other worthwhile purposes. I know that it appears that we finally gained victory some years ago. Yes, we have declared victory and have moved on to other matters. Matters of peace in a world that at last appeared safe from the violence that once plagued us."

Some in the audience appeared restless, their attention lessening.

Mark made several steps forward. "But I am here to tell you that we are not safe!" He vigorously gestured. "Not safe at all."

"You see, I have irrefutable evidence that a new organization exists that is gaining anew weapons of mass destruction. Oh, it is not al Qaeda. As far as I know it is not connected to that defunct organization in any way. But this new group follows much the pattern of al Qaeda, except that it is determined not to make the same mistakes as al Qaeda."

The signs of restlessness in the audience quickly evaporated.

"I am not free to tell you the specific evidence that is in my hands without jeopardizing the lives of men who are completing the dangerous task of obtaining final irrefutable proof. However I can tell you that I have given that evidence to President Knox. Unfortunately, he has failed to act on my warnings. That failure, Ladies and Gentlemen, is why I resigned from the President's cabinet."

Some in the audience gasped at confirmation of the speculation.

"Since I have resigned, I have warned the President of even more evidence, and tonight I warn you that the threat is real. Very real. Indeed, I tell you now, at this moment, the threat is imminent."

Suddenly, Mark was interrupted by a young questioner who stood in the audience. "Proof? What is your proof? You can't expect us to merely accept what you say without specifics. Yes, your proof, sir!" The man appeared to be a student. He wore his hair short and was neatly groomed.

"Hear. Hear," several others shouted unceremoniously in the Oxford Union tradition.

"Yes, let's have your proof," said another skeptic, loudly.

Just then, while Mark was searching for words, the outside door opened. Mark recognized a personal assistant from Worcester College, who came quickly forward. She handed a paper to Mark.

"Excuse me, please," said Mark. "But apparently, something important has come up."

"Please answer the question," the student persisted as Mark read the short note.

> *"Mark, one of my reporters on Tamar has been murdered by the terrorists. The other is hiding in the jungle, but managed to phone me on his mobile. He doesn't respond to my calls. I'm afraid he too has been killed. Christina."*

For a moment Mark felt as if his legs would not hold him. He took a deep breath, gathering his thoughts and then spoke. "You ask for proof. Sadly, the message I have just received releases me from my obligation to keep my proof to myself, and so in a moment I will read this message to you." Mark lifted the note to shoulder height. "Recently I attended a meeting in the offices of *Il Verita*, the newspaper, in Rome. You see the publisher and owner of *Il Verita* has been a long time friend and confidante of mine, Madam Christina Bagliani. Ms. Bagliani has been the source of the information about this new terrorist threat."

Mark's composure began to return as he continued. "In Rome I met with two *Il Verita* investigative reporters who had learned of a terrorist training camp on a remote Southeastern Pacific island nation. An island I had never heard of. At the end of our meeting, the reporters were to return to the island for more information. It was thought that the terrorists were plotting to bomb the United States Embassy in Rome, in addition to bombing several other U.S. embassies throughout the world. Until I received this message . . . " Mark again held up the paper. " . . . I could not disclose these facts. But now, let me read it to you." Mark's legs had steadied under him. Now, he was beginning to feel a swell of anger. It had been only a few days ago that he had been talking to the murdered young man. Or were both now dead? His hand trembled as he read aloud Christina's message.

> *"One of my reporters on Tamar has been murdered. The other is hiding in the jungle, but managed to phone me on his cell phone. He doesn't respond to my calls. I'm afraid he too has been killed."*

Mark lowered the paper. "It is signed by Ms. Bagliani."

The audience murmured.

At that moment Derek Hardin stood and quietly left the building.

Before Mark could ponder Derek's sudden exit, a question came from a young man in the audience. "Do you feel this proves your case?"

"There is no doubt about it, but then, I never had a doubt."

"What do you intend to do about this development?" asked another.

"Yes, do you intend to run for President of your country, sir?" followed still another.

"What I intend to do is to immediately leave for London and fly home to my country. It is vital that the world be awakened to this threat. On my journey to my home I'll have many hours to decide my course of action. But I tell you now, that there will be a course of action. I shall soon make my plans known to the American people."

"But, sir—" said the questioner.

"I'm sorry, but there will be no more questions. It is important that I return home at once."

Murmuring, the crowd began to disperse. Rodney immediately stepped up to Mark. "I want to fly with you. You need a friend—an old friend."

"But what about your hotel deal?"

"Bugger my hotel deal. I want to be with my friend. I'm going with you."

Derek Hardin's car telephone signaled a call. It was Assad. "Sir, my men got him. Both are dead."

"Good," replied Derek. Coming from Derek Hardin this was high praise.

CHAPTER ELEVEN

It was the day after the Oxford Union speech. Mark had spent the night at the Provost's Lodgings. He wanted to read the morning newspapers at breakfast before returning to London. As he had often done as a student, he walked up Walton Street to the newsagent. He bought copies of the *London Daily Telegraph* and the English language edition of *Il Verita International*. Walking back toward the college, he glanced first at the *Daily Telegraph*. On the third page was an item about his speech. It read:

> *"Former U.S. cabinet member warns of renewed terrorist danger."*

He put the paper under his arm, intending to read the complete article at breakfast. Next, Mark looked at *Il Verita*.

> *Il Verita Reporters Reported Murdered*

shouted the front-page headline.

> Il Verita *has received notice from an unidentified source that one and perhaps two of its investigative reporters on Tamar*

> *have been executed by the authorities of that island nation. No other details were made immediately available, nor has Il Verita been able to verify the information. Christina Bagliani, publisher of Il Verita stated: 'At this time Il Verita will not provide the names of the possibly murdered reporters, nor disclose the nature of their confidential mission, other than to say they were working on a story for this newspaper. We hope to have more to report in the very near future.'*

As Mark hurried back to the Provost's Lodgings. he pulled his telephone from his pocket. It would be 6:00 A.M. in Rome, as he punched in Christina's home number.

"Pronto," answered the maid.

"Mrs. Bagliani, please, this is Mr. Stevens."

"Un momento."

"Christina, I've just read the news," said Mark. "Is it true? Are there any new developments? Have both been murdered?"

"I'm certain about one. Probably both are dead. We have received no more telephone calls. Word that both have been killed has come directly from Assad's headquarters. Perhaps from Assad himself." Christina seemed near tears. He had not heard such dismay in her voice since they were young and she had told him she was marrying Otello Bagliani, then owner of *Il Verita*.

"Assad? Who's he?" asked Mark.

"He's their leader. He's the one planning the embassy attacks."

"It seems obvious the murders of your reporters are a warning to the rest of the world," commented Mark. "The message is clear. 'Stay off our island!'"

"What are you planning on doing, Mark? It may be only a matter of days before they start blowing up embassies."

"I'm going to America! Today. Right now. Can you meet me at the Stansted airport? I mean can you be packed and ready to go with me? Rodney wants to go with me and I need you, too, badly."

"The *Il Verita* jet came in from Milano last night. The crew will be ready by the time I get to the airport. Are we going to San Francisco?"

"I've still got to decide. I may go to Washington. There might well be another September 11 and it might be very soon. All hell is going to break loose. I must do whatever I can to wake up my country."

"Whatever you decide, I want to be with you at a time like this."

The jet with Rodney and Christina aboard had just passed over the Scottish coast when Mark connected to President Knox.

"Mark, how the hell are you?" said Knox. "I was told you made some sort of speech at Oxford. Sounds like you're enjoying yourself."

"Stuart. It wasn't just some sort of speech. The publisher of the Italian newspaper I've told you about is on my plane with me. Both of her reporters have been killed by terrorists on Tamar.

"Well, I'm sorry to hear that. Are you sure?"

"Stuart, there's definitely a plot to blow up the United States embassy in Rome—and very likely several of our other embassies—maybe even the Capitol building. God only knows. Mr. President this is serious stuff, as I've been telling you."

"Mark, I appreciate what you're telling me." Knox's tone was soothing. "I'll make sure Homeland and the CIA are on top of this thing."

"Stuart, I want to come to Washington. I think we should have a meeting. I need you to understand—"

"Come on, Mark," the President interrupted. "We've been over this before. There's no need to come to Washington. I've got a campaign trip starting in a few hours. Half a dozen cities out West."

"Then I'll meet with the agency heads," Mark replied. "I'm sure you can arrange it for me."

"No. No," the President responded. "That isn't wise. I'll tell you what. I'll have Harry tell the CIA to call you on your plane. You can fill them in." The President's attitude seemed casual.

"Dammit, Stuart. I don't think I'm getting across to you. This is urgent."

"Mark, I've got people waiting. I hardly had time for your call. I'll have Harry tell Director Ashman, if he's in town, to contact you. Sorry. Mark, but I've got to say goodbye now. Thanks for the call."

President Knox buzzed his secretary. "Mandy, tell Harry I want to see him. Right now."

"What is it, Mr. President?" asked Harry Manning, standing across the Presidential desk from Knox.

"It's Stevens. He just called. He's over the Atlantic someplace. Coming back from England with his damn entourage. He's still got a bee in his bonnet about the threat to our embassies."

"More of that crap, eh?"

"Yeah, some Italian reporters were killed in Tamar or someplace. Probably sticking their noses into some dictator's business. This whole thing is a bunch of overblown bullshit—but it could be delicate. I don't want him going on television, when we've got an election coming up. He wanted to see me here in the oval office. Can you imagine what the press could do with that?"

"Yeah. What did you tell him?"

"I told him you'd have Director Ashman contact him. Get hold of Bob. Tell him to call Stevens. Tell him the risks."

"Political risks, you mean?"

"Yeah. But be careful about it. Ashman doesn't have all that much political savvy. Tell him to treat Mark and his so-called news with respect."

"Okay."

"But don't call him for a couple of days."

The President lit a cigarette.

"You know, Harry, I'm worried. This could blow up in my face. I think Mr. Mark Stevens wouldn't mind being called President Mark Stevens."

"Relax, you're the President. Stevens wouldn't stand a chance of getting the nomination from you."

An hour passed. Mark had left the others and sat alone in his private compartment near the front of the plane. He had been staring out the window, pondering what he should do. Knox wasn't going to do anything.

He knew the likelihood of the CIA director's calling him was close to nil. That was the way Knox operated.

The North Atlantic was covered by clouds. There was nothing to see. That was okay. He wanted to think.

There was a break in the clouds. Greenland came into sight. Mark returned to the rear compartment where the others were.

"We're going to New York."

"New York?" exclaimed Rodney.

"Yes, I want to go to the World Trade Center Memorial. It's important that I be there."

Mark reached Rolf at his law office in Sonoma. It was just after 9:00 in the morning in California. "Rolf, I want you to meet me in New York. Tonight, if you can. You can take one of the company's jets. Can you do it?"

"Of course I can, "Rolf responded. "Obviously it's important."

"I want your advice. I've got to make the most important decision of my life and I don't want to do something stupid or impulsive."

It was the next afternoon in New York. Rolf Williams joined the rest at the Stevens Company co-op apartment near the Metropolitan Museum. Mark had not slept, but he felt no fatigue. Christina, Rodney, Rolf and Mark sat around the large coffee table in the elegant living room overlooking Central Park. Jorge had poured Christina a glass of wine. The others drank mineral water.

"Rolf, I appreciate your coming on short notice.

"I knew it was important," said Rolf.

"You three know me better than any other people on the planet. I want your judgment."

Mark filled Rolf in on the training camp in Tamar and the murder.

"I was in the middle of my speech at Oxford last night, when Christina sent me a message about the killing of her reporter. She's now convinced that both reporters are dead. There's no doubt that the threats to our Rome embassy, and probably other embassies, is very real."

"Then you clearly should warn the authorities. Get a message through to President Knox."

"I've already talked to Knox. He gave me the old Knox brush-off as he has for weeks now. Oh, he protects his ass all right. Says he'll have the CIA contact me. But he's not taking me seriously."

"Why not?"

"I'm not sure why not. He figures he's a cinch for re-election. The economy's in decent shape. No serious foreign affairs problems—at least that are apparent."

"But he wouldn't deliberately expose the country to danger, would he?" asked Rodney.

"He figures I'm an alarmist," Mark responded. "Knox is an intellectual lightweight, but he's a damn good politician. He thinks the voters might get worried about him if they thought there was another terrorist problem on his watch. And, in the last analysis, Knox is just like most everyone else. He thinks the terrorists have been long since defeated. Everybody—we're back to the way we were before the September 11 attack back in 2001."

"So then, what do you plan to do?" Rolf asked.

"I'm thinking of running for President. What do you think of that idea?"

"I think you'd make a damn good President. But I also think your chances are about as close to zero as you can get." Rolf got up and walked to the window, staring at Central Park. He turned abruptly to his friend. "You certainly can't run as a Democrat, although that might be the Democrat's best chance to beat Knox. Knox is a tremendous politician. Well liked."

"I don't pretend to understand American politics," said Rodney. "But wouldn't you have to win practically all the Republican primaries? Although from what I've read nearly all the primaries are on the same date now."

"True," said Mark. "But I—"

"You're not going to get the nomination away from a popular sitting President," interrupted Rolf. "Even Ronald Reagan couldn't do that way back when Ford was President."

"I assume you're right," said Christina. "But Mark has to do something."

"Of course," said Rolf. "That's the way he's always been. Can't sit idly by."

"Look friends. That's why I wanted to talk to each of you. You see, I don't really expect to be President."

"You don't?" asked Rolf. "Then exactly what do you want?"

"I want to warn—no, I want to wake up this country. We are in great danger and no one wants to hear it."

Rolf, who had resumed his chair opposite Mark, continued. "Look, Mark. Maybe it'll take the blowing up of an embassy or two to wake up this country. After all, it took the World Trade Center the first time." He got up again and paced around the room with the others watching. "What I'm saying is, I'm not sure that one voice in the wilderness can do it. Not sure at all. Listen, are you certain it's not just your restlessness that makes you want to try this lesson in futility?"

"You're saying I shouldn't run then?"

"No I'm saying you shouldn't run just because of your restlessness—your ambition, if you will. You're too old for that. Hopefully, Mark, too wise. You've got to have a reason above all the stuff that drives most politicians."

Quietly sitting in his chair Rodney broke his silence. "My dear Rolf, I very well know your heart is in the right place. Sorry, but I disagree with you. Let me tell you some of my personal history, if I may."

Rolf resumed his seat near the large coffee table as he listened to Rodney continue. "When I first met our friend here, I was a fat, pointless son of a Lord. My destiny? To get a gentleman's Third at Oxford. To live the life of the gentleman—a time honored English tradition. I had no enthusiasm for anything. But then I met a man named Mark Stevens. He had ambition. His life had purpose. His life was exciting. I wanted to be like him—at least to the best of my poor ability. I became successful in my own right and it made me a happy man—happier than any man has a right to be." The others listened intently. "If Mark's restlessness leads him to make a run at the Presidency, then so be it. It is that very restlessness that makes great men. And, at the risk of embarrassing our friend here, I say he is a great man and destined for even greater greatness."

Christina spoke. "I think you already know my feelings. I say go for it! This terrorism is serious. You've got to do everything you can to stop it."

Mark smiled. He was silently somewhat amused by the psychological analyses of him by his well-meaning longtime friends. He supposed each had some truth in it. But to hell with it! He had made up his mind. "You all flatter me. I appreciate your advice. I've made my decision. I want to make a speech at the World Trade Center Memorial tomorrow afternoon in time to make the evening news. Rodney, I want you to call my San Francisco offices. Have them alert the television people. The same with the press. Announce it on the Internet. Everyone you can think of. Make arrangements to get some campaign advisors—someone to help me with the primaries. I don't expect to win, but we're going to get my message across. Or I should say my messages, plural. Might as well lay out all my beliefs. I'm no longer a member of the President's cabinet. I can say what I damned well want to."

CHAPTER TWELVE

The limo let Mark, Christina, Rolf, and Rodney out at the curb of the busy downtown Manhattan street. Mark looked in awe at the many post 2001 buildings surrounding the site of the World Trade Center memorial to the September 11, 2001 attack. The buildings and streets were occupied by the everyday business of a new population, one who had no fear of danger from terrorists and most of whom knew of nine-eleven as merely an historical event, often seen over the years on television with the planes crashing into the towers and the collapse of the gigantic twin towers into clouds of dust.

There had been no time for crews to put his speech on the teleprompters. Mark would have to speak with only a few notes. He doubted if he would need them anyway, for his message was clear in his mind.

While the television people were adjusting their equipment, a hastily summoned makeup artist dabbed at his face. "Ready, Mr. Stevens," commanded an unseen person from behind a camera. It had been a scant 15 minutes since he had left the limo.

Mark took a deep breath and began. Although there had been little time for the networks to announce his speech, he knew that millions would see him on sound bites on various news programs this evening and tomorrow.

"Ladies and Gentlemen. Last night I arrived from England on a hastily planned journey of importance to us all. It is altogether appropriate that I speak to you of this serious matter from the World Trade Center site here on Manhattan." Mark paused. He greatly wanted to make an effective speech. He had appeared on television many times, yet he felt a wave of uncertainty as to how to deliver his all important message.

"For months before resigning as Secretary of the Treasury, I have been warning the President of a new threat of terrorism. I have warned our Congress that the threat was real and imminent. I was dismayed that my warnings went unheeded. Apparently your government feels that since September 11, 2001, adequate steps have been taken to protect the nation from further terrorist attacks. I vigorously disagree." Mark paused, looking at a different camera. "Our government has fallen asleep to a dangerous threat." Mark gestured and turned back to the main TV camera. "You are not going to like what I am about to say, but it is time for the truth—time we all in this country faced the truth. Our nation has permitted itself to be lulled into a false sense of safety. I am not only speaking of both political parties, I am speaking of you, the American people. Why do I think the threat is real and imminent? Because I have evidence! Compelling evidence!

"To tell you of such evidence I will introduce you to my friend of over 40 years—Christina Bagliani. Ms. Bagliani is the owner and publisher of the authoritative and respected worldwide Rome based newspaper *Il Verita*. Some months ago it was Ms. Bagliani who provided me with certain information upon which I based my warnings to the President and the Congress. Ms. Bagliani has flown from Rome today to help me warn you of the imminent threat we all face. My fellow citizens, I give you Ms. Christina Bagliani."

Christina took her place at the clump of microphones. Despite her conservative black dress, her beauty was striking. Mark could see that her hands were trembling as she began her remarks, completely without notes. At that moment Mark knew that he not only loved Christina, but that he was proud of her. They were both so different from when they had fallen in love 40 years ago. Now they loved each other with a much different and stronger love.

Christina's gentle Italian accent added an aura of interest as she began.

"Ladies and Gentlemen, of the American audience I am honored to speak to you. Although I am Italian. Born there. Grew up there. And now live in Rome, where I am the owner and publisher of *Il Verita*. For several years as a young woman, I lived in California. Although fate took me back to my homeland, it was in California that I fell in love with America." Mark saw that Christina's hands no longer trembled. "And I still love America." Christina smiled gently. "You see, when an Italian woman falls in love, she never forgets."

Christina turned to face the second television camera. "The world rallied around America after September 11, 2001. *Il Verita* consistently supported the actions America took to defend itself, even though some of those actions were not popular in Europe. After all it has always been the United States, and not Italy, that was the likely target of terrorists and rogue nations."

Christina returned to face to the main camera. "But as Mark—I should say Secretary Stevens—has said in the past several years, the world and even America has become complacent. I stand here to tell you that the terrorist threat is still very much with us. Several months ago *Il Verita* learned that forces of evil had taken control of the small South Pacific nation of Tamar. Following up on a lead, my newspaper had its two best investigative reporters pose as individuals disaffected with the Italian government and with America. They were recruited by the leader of Tamar and sent to that island nation for training in the techniques of destruction. They soon learned of a plot to blow up certain American embassies in various countries. They were assigned the task of leading an attack on the American embassy at Via Veneto in Rome. Throughout the investigation, I notified Secretary Stevens of these activities. It was based upon my information that he, in turn, privately warned President Knox and later the American Congress.

"Not long ago these brave young reporters, Mario and Roberto, met with me and Secretary Stevens in my offices in Rome. I decided to hold the story, breaking the news of the threat until they had made one more trip to Tamar to gather conclusive proof of the plan to blow up the embassies. That is a decision that I regret. It proved to be disastrous. You see, yesterday we learned that both Mario and Roberto had been murdered in Tamar. As you Americans say, murdered in cold blood, upon the orders of a man named Assad. Assad is the leader behind the throne in Tamar. I have verified these killings." Christina wiped away tears as she spoke of the murders. "I'm sorry I am unable to continue, except to say Mark Stevens is the one leader who truly understands that the threat of terrorism is no longer merely a threat. The world, and that means America, must act before it is too late. Before your embassies are blown up—and perhaps even worse."

As Christina spoke, Mark realized more than ever how much he admired Christina. He left his chair and stood behind Christina at the bank of microphones. His affection and compassion for Christina was clear to all watching as he stroked her arm and helped her to her chair before returning to the microphones himself.

Mark noticed that there were more people in the television crews than there were listening to them speak. He certainly hoped that more would be watching on TV.

"Americans. The question is, then, 'Why am I telling you all this?' Or better put: 'What am I going to do about all this?' I have tried to persuade President Knox. Many times before I resigned from his cabinet. He won't listen. Oh, he pretends to listen, but ignores the facts. Only yesterday while over the Atlantic I spoke to the President. It is obvious that even with these new developments, he doesn't take the threat seriously. I dislike saying this. But this is an election year. He wants a second term, badly. And he doesn't want to rock any boats." Mark was speaking heatedly. He didn't give a damn. He was telling the truth. "And what about Congress," he continued. "I've testified before Congress about this, but nothing is done." Mark ignored his few notes and looked intently at the camera. "My fellow Americans, I am going to run for President! That is what I am going to do about this!" Mark instinctively paused for effect. "I'm announcing today that I'm entering the Republican primaries! I intend to win the Republican nomination for President of the United States!" There were a few gasps from the seasoned television crew. "There are many issues in this coming election. Our taxes are too high. I believe in a two tier flat tax. Second, I believe in a different immigration policy. Third, I believe we should consider uniting with the European Union. Another, I believe in a different Federal Reserve policy. I have many ideas that might well shake up the same old political debate we all have become used to." Mark again shifted to the second camera. "But all these issues are like nothing compared to the main issue. The issue of terrorism. We must wake up America. We must stop this threat—this very real threat—in its tracks before our embassies are blown up. And before, God only knows, whatever else is brewing in the minds of this new, yet old, group of madmen." Mark paused, gathering his breath. "And so tomorrow I'm flying to Iowa. I intend to win the Iowa Republican caucus and then on to New Hampshire where I intend to win again. And then, on the first Tuesday in February when all the remaining state primaries are to be held, I intend to win enough delegates to assure myself of the Republican nomination for the Presidency." Continuing to look intently at the camera, Mark wrapped up his speech. "And so, my fellow Americans, that is what I shall do about this terrorism threat. I intend to win your support. I intend to be your next President. Good night."

There was no applause as Mark left the camera area. Some of the few spectators appeared to be talking to one another in subdues tones as they left the area.

CHAPTER THIRTEEN

That night Mark's jet was over the Midwest, headed for Iowa and its caucuses. Some years ago each state that had primary elections for delegates to the Democrat and Republican conventions had agreed with their respective national committees to hold their elections on the first Tuesday of February—not earlier—not later. That is, all states except New Hampshire and Iowa. Each of the two insisted on retaining their traditional prideful positions as bell-weather states. As always Iowa did not hold an actual primary, but retained its somewhat puzzling system of party caucuses that selected Iowa's delegates to the national conventions—for the Republicans, this year to be held in Los Angeles. Mark was to speak tomorrow to the caucus in Des Moines.

Rodney, Christina, Rolf, and Mark gathered around the TV to watch the reaction of the political pundits to his speech at the World Trade Center. Rolf switched from channel to channel. It was all negative. "The terrorist threat is nonsense," said one commentator. "It's an issue of the past," opined another. The major national news broadcasts did not even cover the speech, while some, only briefly mentioning it.

When Rolf finally snapped off the TV, Mark spoke first: "It's disappointing, I know. But I hardly expected them to put me on their shoulders and carry me to the White House. It's not the White House I want anyway. I want to get the message to the people. I want whoever wins the White House to know my slogan 'terrorism is back!' My challenge is to convince the American people, so that they demand that the other candidates wake up."

"Yes, but how?" Rolf responded.

"By persuading them—starting with Iowa!" answered Rodney.

"I don't think that Mark will be the only persuader," commented Christina."

"Well, then, who else?" asked Rolf."

"Assad will do it. Long before the conventions," said Christina with resolve. "He'll attack the American embassies. That will wake everyone up."

"But what a heavy price to pay," Mark responded with a grim expression. "I've got to do better in Des Moines tomorrow."

* * *

But in London Derek Hardin sat alone in his office. He had just watched Mark's World Trade Center speech replayed on the BBC morning news. Derek was surprised, yet not surprised. Surprised, because when it came to business decisions, he knew that Stevens had always looked hard logic in the face. Surely, Stevens knew he didn't stand a chance at the American Presidency. But not surprised, because he knew from experience that once Mark Stevens made up his mind, he never gave up, no matter what the odds. Derek had expected Mark's announcement to seek the Presidency when he had heard him talk at the Oxford Union.

Derek rang his p.a. "I'm going for a drive. Tell Hans that I want the car to be at the side door."

"When, sir?"

"Now!" His face had reddened. "Don't you hear me? For God's sake, do I have to explain everything? Right now!"

Derek charged out of his private elevator to his waiting Maybach. "I want to go to Oxford," he barked to Hans. He turned off his telephone and fax systems. He wanted to think. He needed to decide what to do.

In an hour the big car pulled to a stop in front of Worcester College. Derek was frustrated. Usually decisions came quickly to him, but not this time. He walked past the staircase where Mark, Rodney and he had had rooms as students at Oxford years ago. He sat on the top step of the outdoor stairs leading down to the grassy quad in front of the building, trying to think. But it was no use— too many students walking by—too many memories of past confrontations with Mark Stevens. Before long he was sitting on a bench overlooking the Worcester's lake a hundred yards or so from the college's buildings. There were no students around—only a few ducks in the lake. He thought once again about the hatred he had developed for the United States. It began when, as a youngster, his mother had followed her lover to America and had taken him to live in America—far away from his father, friends and everything he had ever known. Those were wrenching times that had been forever implanted in his psyche. He watched the ducks paddle in the lake, making an occasional quack. His mind again reverted to his many confrontations with Mark Stevens. Confrontations that began in the Nag's Head pub when the news spread that America's President Kennedy had been assassinated. Stevens had knocked Derek to the floor when Derek voiced his unpopular opinion about the young President. His hatred had recently arisen again when Mark Stevens, as U.S. Treasury Secretary, thwarted his attempt to buy an American bank. An hour passed before he rose from the bench. He had made up his mind. He had his plan.

As the large Maybach sped back to London on the M40 motorway, Derek telephoned Assad in Tamar.

"I want you to call off the bombings of the American embassies," he told his confederate.

"What? Everything is all set. What are you talking about?" Assad demanded. "We've been working on this for months!"

Derek tried to repress his anger at Assad's effrontery. He needed Assad as much as Assad needed him and his money. "Because the bombing would play right into Stevens's hands," Derek answered sternly. "Don't you see? Bombings would arouse the American public. They would have to take Stevens seriously. It might even catapult him into the Presidency. Bloody hell, the last thing I want is an aroused American public with Stevens as President. Call off the bombings for now. I want Stevens to look like a fool for predicting the embassy bombings. There will be a better time to make our move."

"It had better be soon," answered Assad. "We've got cells in six countries all ready for action. I don't want my people to think I'm weak."

"Tell them there will be greater things to come. You can handle it. After all, you are their leader."

"I repeat, it had better be soon!"

"I want you to call off the bombings and come to London immediately. We need to sort this out face to face." Abruptly Derek ended the call. Without his money, Assad could do nothing. Derek was in charge and he knew it.

Hardin's mind was whirring as the Maybach drove into London's financial district. He had made still another decision. His private elevator whisked him to his office.

"Robert, come in here. I want to talk to you about a very important matter," Derek ordered his assistant. "And don't let Elizabeth know I'm meeting with you. Come in through the conference room." Derek was referring to Elizabeth Cannon, his other prime assistant.

"Sit down, Robert. I've got something of utmost importance to tell you. And, of course, it must be kept confidential from everyone else. There must be no leaks— absolutely none. Do you understand?"

Mystified, Robert Marsden sat opposite Derek's pretentious desk. He and Elizabeth had carried out many dark assignments from Hardin. What could this be? And why was she excluded?

"I want to tell you about my venture in Tamar—and it's not about oil."

"Yes, sir," said Robert, obediently.

"First of all, I want to tell you that your salary will be tripled, from one million pounds to three million pounds. You will be involved in a very delicate and secret mission. I will pay you the extra two million from my personal account. There must be no record of it. No one must suspect. Do you understand?"

"Why, yes, sir. I do understand. You are very generous, sir."

"I am not being overly generous. When you hear what I have to say. You will see that you will be earning every bit of it."

Marsden leaned forward in anticipation. What was this secret?

When Derek finished with the true story of his adventures in Tamar, Marsden blanched. Hardin had been involved in many questionable deals, but this was beyond the pale. Yet, three million pounds per year! What was he supposed to do to earn such a princely sum?

"You see, Robert, in recent months all this has come to involve my old enemy, Mark Stevens. He has heard about the plan to destroy the embassies. But since he could not convince the American President that it was true, Stevens has announced that he is going to run for President himself."

"I see," said Marsden, his mouth agape.

"And, he must be stopped!"

"But he doesn't stand a chance, does he? At the Presidency—"

"Not since I called off the bombings, but—"

"You called them off, sir?"

"Yes, an hour ago. All they would accomplish is to alert the Americans to the fact that Stevens knew what he was talking about. God knows, it might even bloody well get him elected."

"I see. But what are you going to do?"

"That is where you come in, Robert."

"But what am I to do?"

I want you to infiltrate into the Stevens camp. And I want you to help with this whole Assad operation. We need a spy. We need to know where Stevens is vulnerable— what his specific plans are—where he intends to appear in public. He must be stopped before he arouses the sleeping American giant. That's all for now. We'll talk in more detail as soon as I've made more decisions."

Stunned, Marsden left the room. He would do whatever was asked of him. Three million pounds. He smiled. Besides, the whole thing sounded very exciting. He had yearned for more excitement for some time now.

Derek waited until Marsden had left the offices. "Elizabeth, would you come into my office? Come in through the conference room, I don't want anyone to know we're meeting."

"Yes, sir. Most everyone has left the office anyway."

Elizabeth Cannon sat in a chair opposite Derek's desk. She was wearing her usual short skirt and high heels. She was a very attractive woman, indeed. Derek got up from behind his desk and seated himself in one of the two couches that faced one another. "Please sit in the other sofa," Derek said, motioning. "I have something serious to talk to you about."

Elizabeth did as requested, carefully crossed her legs and pulled her skirt down as far as it would go. In these years working for Hardin, he had never made any advances toward her, but this late afternoon, the possibility crossed her mind. She was apprehensive.

She was soon to learn that while her apprehension was justified, it was for an entirely different reason.

"You are aware of my frequent trips to Tamar?" he asked.

"Yes—the oil venture."

"In fact, Elizabeth, the oil deal is merely a cover."

"A cover, sir?" She stiffened, wondering what revelation was coming next.

Derek launched into the whole story of the new al Qaeda plot.

When he finished, Elizabeth was astounded. "But, what is my role supposed to be?" she blurted out in amazement.

"Before we get to that, I want to tell you that as of this moment I am raising your salary from one million pounds to three million. The extra two million will be paid from my personal account. No one but I will know and that includes Robert Marsden. I know you work closely with him. He is not to know of your new role."

Still flabbergasted, Elizabeth veritably whispered: "And what, sir, will be my role?"

"Elizabeth, you are a very attractive woman—very attractive indeed. I want you to use your attributes to help my cause."

"I don't understand, Mr. Hardin, what is it that I'm to do and how would this aid your—." She searched for the correct word. "Cause."

"I want you to go to America. I want you to be involved in Stevens's campaign for President. I want you to get close to this man. I've known him for many years. He is very attracted to beautiful women. I need someone close to him—perhaps privy to his plans. I don't know exactly what you are to do—what you are to find out. But it will all unfold in due course. It would be disastrous to me if he were elected President, or even if he only succeeded in arousing the government to my plans. Do you understand?

"Yes, sir. I believe I understand. But I don't know how you expect me to help you." She was flabbergasted by what she had heard.

"I believe you do Elizabeth. I do believe you understand very well. It's a matter of getting inside information from Mark Stevens, or at least someone high up in his campaign."

Elizabeth gulped, mystified, yet vaguely understanding what might be expected.

"This is something Marsden could not do. Don't you see it takes an attractive woman such as you?"

Elizabeth's skirt had crept up a bit as they talked. She, as casually as she could, pulled it back down. The situation made her very ill at ease.

"Now if you like, we can go to my club for dinner and discuss it further."

She hesitated. "That would be delightful, sir, but I'm sorry I've been invited to the opera at Covent Garden." She gulped again; in all these years Derek had never invited her to dinner.

Elizabeth left the offices in bewilderment—a state of mind new to her. She hailed a taxi rather than taking the underground to her flat. Riding in the cab, she pondered a serious question. Three million pounds was a great deal of money. The two extra million would be tax free—unreported. After only one year she could quit her position and be forever freed of this unpleasant man. But exactly what was being asked of her? In the extreme was she expected to use sex to accomplish the tasks set out for her? She was no prude, but she had never gone to bed with anyone she didn't have strong feelings for. Certainly she had known for years that her attractiveness to men had led to her getting ahead in the business world. She had to admit it had even been helpful, to at least some degree, in her success at Oxford's Queen's College, where she had earned a First—the highest of grades. More than one of the dons had invited her to share a lager. But to trade explicit sexual favors for a huge salary? That was something she doubted she was willing to do. Yet—well—she had some thinking to do.

From her flat, she telephoned her date. "Sorry, but I'm having to work late. I'm afraid I must cancel the opera. I'm very, very, sorry, but I just cannot leave the office."

Elizabeth doubted that she would get much sleep tonight.

CHAPTER FOURTEEN

The crowd in the Des Moines, Iowa meeting hall was dismally small, less than 50 curious people. President Knox's press secretary had announced he intended to skip both the Iowa caucuses and the New Hampshire primary—that he was too busy with his Presidential duties. It was obvious to most that he did not take Mark's candidacy seriously.

Mark decided that he had to make the best of the dismal turnout. The saving grace was that several newspaper reporters were there and one of the national news cable channels had showed up with cameras. Perhaps he could get out his message through the media. One of the hastily selected campaign staff pointed out to Mark that a well-known blog writer was in the group, also.

Mark began by moving through the small group shaking hands. "I'd like you to meet my friends," he said to each person, telling them the names of Christina, Rodney, and Rolf. "Christina is the publisher of the international newspaper *Il Verita*. She was the person who brought to my attention this new terrorist threat."

Mark gave special attention to the media representatives. When he finished chatting with the group he moved to the podium, where he ignored the lectern, and moved about without a microphone as he spoke to the audience. He had removed his suit jacket and loosened his tie.

"Ladies and Gentlemen, you and people like you hold the future of this country in your hands." Mark decided to make his speech short and directly to the point. He wanted to keep their attention. "Stuart Knox does not take the terrorist threat seriously. He'd rather be re-elected than admit that he has ignored my many warnings. Including another try two days ago. He's afraid to admit to this newly discovered problem. Afraid you will realize that he has made no serious effort to stop the imminent threat to our overseas embassies and not re-nominate him for a second term. I assure you that once these bombing occur, the next threat will be to targets here in the United States." Mark went on to explain the role of the *Il Verita* reporters, their discoveries and their murders. "This threat is real and will be carried out. My campaign is to wake up Americans to the threat, and whomever is elected President in November, be it Republican or Democrat. You, the Republicans of Iowa can help me in my cause by voting for me in your caucuses. Even if you believe I don't have a chance, your vote for me is important. It will send a message." Mark paused. There was no applause, no response from the silent Iowans. "You see, it is not important that I be the next President. What is important is that the next President do something about this new terrorist threat.

"Now I'll try to answer your questions."

At first there seemed to be no questions, but then a man wearing a farmer's overalls spoke. "I suppose you may be right in your pessimistic predictions about terrorism, but I'm worried about other things too."

"Yes," Mark answered. "Fire away."

"What is your stance on farm subsidies? The corn subsidy for one."

"You, sir, want a straight answer, I assume. You strike me as that sort of fellow," said Mark.

"I do. Straight from the shoulder. Man to man."

"Well, sir, I am opposed to subsidies. Subsidies of any type, throughout the whole economy. Farm programs and subsidies were originally designed to help out the individual small farmer. The small American farmer, eking out a living on, say 80 acres, was a way of life that Congress wanted to keep. And, by the way, to get the farmers' votes. But that was in the 1930s. Today much, even most, farming is done by big corporations. Even the individual farmers typically farm a thousand acres, or even more. This is not the way of life that taxpayers should be paying for. It has become a political matter. Politicians are afraid to touch the issue. They don't want to lose your vote."

"Well, Mr. Stevens, you have lost my vote for sure," rejoined the man. "Even if you're right about the embassy attacks. We survived September 11th. And we can survive an attack on a few foreign embassies—if it happens, which I doubt."

"I'm sorry, sir. It's a good thing we don't have many government buildings in Iowa."

The man turned his back on Mark and stomped from the room.

"Are there any other questions?" Mark asked after the man had left.

"Yes, I have a question," a nicely dressed woman said. "What is your stance on abortion?"

"My stance on abortion. Any stance I might have pales in comparison to the issue of terrorism. Terrorism is why I'm running for President. I don't think my stance on abortion is important."

"I think it is," answered the woman. "Are you refusing to answer my question?"

"No, I am not refusing. I'll try to answer any relevant question."

"And you don't think abortion is relevant?"

"Personally I'm in favor of the women's right to choose what they do with their own bodies. But I'm not sure a President has the ability to change the present law, even to suit people who disagree. Perhaps only in the very long run, by his power to appoint Supreme Court Justices—with Senate approval."

"Even to prevent the murder of the unborn?" asked the woman, defiantly.

"In my opinion it is not murder any more than using birth control to prevent a child is murder. But that's my opinion. I respect your right to disagree. This is an issue that has plagued our country for years and one that I think should be left alone in a political campaign. An issue that is ruining the Republican party."

"I certainly disagree with you."

"Look, Maam there is an important point you may be overlooking."

"And what exactly is that?" She was clearly perturbed.

"Let's say Roe v. Wade is reversed. All that would mean is the individual states have a right to ban abortion.

That wouldn't mean that states must ban abortion. Do you think for one minute like, say the states of California and New York would ban abortion? No way. A young woman in Iowa, if Iowa outlawed abortion, could go to a state where abortion is legal. Or in a worse case go to an illegal abortion clinic here in Des Moines."

"Gee, I never realized that. But I guess I'd still be opposed to abortion."

"That would be your choice."

Another man spoke up. "Well, Mr. Stevens, an issue that is important to me is this gay rights business. How do you stand on gay rights?"

"Again, an issue that has no place in a Presidential election."

"It's an issue important to me!" the man said.

"Very well, I'll tell you my opinion," Mark answered reluctantly. "I have some gay friends. I have no problem with them. But, as I've told those same friends, I'm annoyed by these so-called gay rights marches. In my opinion they do more harm to gays than good. The same is true of demonstrations of other minority groups—ones that continually assert rights. People of all races, religions and beliefs already have the rights they're demonstrating about. Furthermore, I happen to believe that most of the members of these minority groups are annoyed by these marches and demonstrations. We're supposed to be one nation. Not a nation of groups who dislike one another."

The man in the audience spoke up again, "I read that you are unmarried. Tell me, are you gay, sir?"

"I'm not sure that it's any of your business, but my wife was killed in a horrible hotel fire many years ago.

A fire that I barely survived myself, after trying to save her." Mark paused. The memory of Pris's death in the fire caused him to choke up. "Now, I hope that satisfies you and your irrelevant mean-spirited questions! That's all the questions I have time or patience to take! I came here to wake you up to the terrorist threat!"

Mark started to leave the podium. "Mr. Stevens!" another man spoke up. "I want to assure you that these questions certainly do not represent a typical Iowan. I want to tell you that you have won my vote."

"Thank you, sir," Mark answered. "At least that's one." Mark started to leave the stage.

"Even if I disagree with you," the man continued. "I want a Republican candidate who stands up for what he believes. A strong man who sticks to his beliefs. Not just another politician."

"Thank you, sir. I hope there are many more like you."

Mark's plane left for New Hampshire. "Well, what's the verdict?" he asked his friends and the three newly hired political advisors.

"I'm not happy about the situation," said one of the advisors.

"I'm not either," answered Mark. "I don't think I did a good job of getting across my message—the terrorism threat and that alone."

"Oh, you did all right on that score. Trouble is, it wasn't important to the listeners. And you were awfully direct on the other issues. I wish you would avoid them. Somehow."

"But how could I? They asked the questions and I answered them."

"Maybe you should have taken lessons from Stuart Knox. He's good at telling audiences what they want to hear. And, it's always got him elected. After all, he's President."

Mark walked to the back of the plane to be amongst his friends. "God, I feel depressed," he told them.

Rolf spoke. "I've seen you depressed before, but you've always snapped out of it and come back fighting."

"But this time I'm not sure I know how to do it," responded Mark.

Christina spoke. "Just keep up what you've done so far. If they don't get the message, it's their problem, not yours." She leaned over and touched Mark's hand.

"I agree," said Rodney. "It's why advertisers on the tellie run the same message over and over. Finally it will sink in."

"Yeah, I suppose so," said Mark, putting his head in his hands. "Maybe I should start making some TV commercials," he concluded, looking up morosely. "Let's make one or two courtesy appearances in New Hampshire and then get on to New York and tape some commercials before the February primaries." Mark's lack of enthusiasm was palpable to all.

As they exited the plane outside the terminal at the Manchester, New Hampshire airport, a messenger approached them. "Is there a Mrs. Bagliani here?"

"Yes, I'm Christina Bagliani." As often when she was stressed her Italian accent was very pronounced.

The messenger handed a note to Christina. The air was bitter cold and she had difficulty opening the folded sheet of paper. "Contact the newspaper at once. Mario has survived will be in Rome."

Christina staggered a bit and reached for Mark's arm. "What is it Christina?" Mark asked.

"Apparently Mario has escaped from Tamar. We thought he was dead! They want me to call at once!"

"My God," uttered Mark. "Let's get back in the plane where it's warm. You can call from there."

"Mario somehow survived. He's been in the hospital for a check-up. They expect him at *Il Verita* tomorrow." Christina hung up the phone.

"Amazing!" said Mark.

"Mark, I've got to return to Rome!"

"I understand. You can use my plane. They'll leave as soon as they refuel, if you like."

"I'll find out if my plane is still at Stansted."

"No matter. We'll get you to Rome."

"No need. I'll have them send my plane to London. Then take it to Rome."

Inside the terminal, Mark broke the news to Rolf and Rodney.

"Mark, if you don't mind, I'd better go back with her. To be honest with you," said Rodney. "I've been worried about the hotel deal. I'd better meet with the sellers before they change their minds."

"By all means," Mark answered. "I'm a big boy." The truth was, Mark felt let down. He didn't feel much like such a big boy after the disaster in Des Moines. He needed some time to get his enthusiasm back, "I'm going back to the plane to say goodbye to Christina," Mark said. "What an amazing event. Mario still alive, after all."

"Well, my dear, obviously I'm pleased that Mario has survived," said Mark sitting in one of the parked plane's leather chairs, facing Christina.

"Yes, what a shock. I'm anxious to talk to him to find out how he managed."

Mark leaned across and took both her hands. "I had hoped we could make love tonight at the hotel. With all that's happened these past few days, we—"

"I understand, bello," she responded affectionately. There hasn't been time for anything but politics." They both stood and he embraced her.

"I guess not, and now this," he whispered. They still held one another.

"It's all right. I know you still love me."

"All I wanted to do was warn the country. Wake up everyone," he said as they both sat down. I have no desire to be President.

"I know. There will be time for us, when all this is over." She felt that Mark seemed a little depressed.

She sat in his lap and kissed him warmly, although not passionately.

Mark had wanted tonight to be as much like the old days as possible, but now that was not to be. He would miss Christina more than ever. Events always seemed to keep them apart. He had to admit that going without her feminine presence in his life left a big hole in his heart, especially when they had been together as much as they had in the last few days. Yet there was nothing he could do about it.

Rolf and Mark watched in the cold night as the plane took off with Christina and Rodney aboard. "It looks as if this New Hampshire campaign is going to be more lonely than I expected," Mark mumbled.

"You'll be all right. You always are in the end."

"I guess so. I need a good night's sleep before the so-called rally tomorrow."

CHAPTER FIFTEEN

"Mark, I think it would be a good idea for me to go down to New York City with the two campaign advisors and begin to make arrangements for your TV clips for the big primaries in February. I'll see if you can get on some talk shows. What do you think?" asked Rolf at breakfast the next morning. "Your schedule for the next two weeks here in New Hampshire is pretty well set."

"Makes sense to me," Mark responded. "Actually, we've got some volunteers who can help me out with hotels, meeting places... you know, all the details."

"You have a bunch of appearances in New Hampshire with the first and last speech scheduled for here in Manchester. Do you know what you're going to say?"

"Pretty much the same as in Des Moines. I hope to hell it's with better results."

"Actually the polls show people were impressed with the candid way you answered questions. It should go better here."

"I'm going to call Christina, to see what happened with her reporter, Mario."

"I've been thinking. If we can get him to New York for the TV ads, it might be pretty spectacular. Could make a big difference," said Rolf.

"No doubt about it."

Mark waited until it was evening in Italy and called Christina. "I saw Mario in the hospital," she said. "He'll be fine in a couple of days. He slipped out of Tamar on a little boat. More of a raft, I gather.

Got picked up by an Indonesian freighter and flew back here from Jakarta. I don't know the details."

"Do you think you can fly him to New York? He would be living proof of what's going on. You know, back me up."

"I'm certain that I can. I will. But, Mark, I'm going to have to stay here in Rome for some time. The newspaper you know. It's hectic here."

"I understand." Although Mark supposed he did understand, he wished she could be with him. He wasn't looking forward to this campaign—not at all—especially without her and without Rodney and Rolf.

Again President Knox declined to participate in the New Hampshire town discussions. "Too busy with affairs of state," the White House announced.

When Mark finished his Manchester speech that night, he opened the floor to questions.

"If you are elected, what do you intend to do about the disparity of wealth between the working class and the wealthy?" asked the first questioner. "I understand you are a billionaire and most of us here in New Hampshire work for a living."

"How do you think I was successful? Mark asked rhetorically. "I worked for a living, just like millions of others. After all, I started out cleaning out winery vats when I was a kid. But to go to the heart of your question, I'm not so much concerned about the so-called disparity as I am about the plight of the poor in our nation and, just as important, about the problem of the shrinking middle class. I don't care about the fact that many people are rich. I wish everyone were rich. The rich pay 90 to 95 percent of the income taxes. The rich give 90 percent of the non-church related charitable giving. The rich invest in our economy, creating businesses and jobs."

"All right then, Mr. Smart Guy, how about the rest of us?"

"Forgive me for coming across as a smart guy, but you touched a button with me.

"However, to go more to your question—the answer is education. Liberal arts education—sure—but not everyone is cut out for college. We need more and better science and technical education. Teach our people to be air conditioning mechanics. Teach them to be plumbers. Teach them to be a variety of technical occupations. Honorable occupations. And—this is vital—teach them to be reliable. Teach them how to run a business—to show up when they said they would show up. Teach them to do a good job at whatever they do. In other words, to be responsible. Teach them—well I don't know—to be successful at whatever they do. Not everyone is likely to be a billionaire—but everyone can be successful at what they do," Mark paused. "But I'm here to tell you that having a billion doesn't necessarily lead to happiness. I suppose I could go on and on."

"Please don't. You've made your point. I'm not sure I agree with you, but I hear you. Give me a billion dollars and I could be happy."

"Are you sure, my friend? Don't be so sure."

Another questioner in the group raised his hand. "Speaking of money, sir, some people say you are using your money to buy the nomination, because you're paying all your own campaign expenses. They say it might be 100 million before it's all over."

"I'll tell you, spending your own money on a campaign is no sin. No one can buy the Presidency no matter how much money he'll spend. Take a look at President Knox. Does being a Congressman and then a Senator for years, having a charming personality, saying the right things, not vetoing pork barrel spending, knowing how to raise money—are all these things supposed to make a candidate a better man than a person like me? A man who was successful in business, who knows how to run a business? If I am attempting to buy the Presidency, then so is every successful politician, in his own way attempting to buy the Presidency!"

There was a smattering of applause. "I never thought of it that way," said the questioner.

"Do you expect us to take this terrorist issue seriously? What proof do you have?" asked another man in the audience.

"I'll tell you this," Mark said. "I just found out that one of the two newsmen we all thought dead, has been reported to have survived.

"I plan to have him come to New York. He'll be on TV telling what he knows about the plot on American Embassies. I expect those interviews will convince the voters in the upcoming February 3rd primaries."

The next morning Mark left Manchester for the trip to Concord, New Hampshire, where he was to speak at a gathering of Republican voters. A car and a volunteer driver picked him up outside his hotel. "Hello, Mr. Stevens, my name is Elizabeth, Elizabeth Cannon. I'm to be your driver whilst you are campaigning here in New Hampshire." She had opened the rear car door for him.

"You're a volunteer?"

"Yes, your talk last night was very good. And I'm certain you can tell by my accent, I'm English." They began their drive.

"Of course, but I'm amazed. What brought you here from England?"

"Well, sir, I was in Oxford when you spoke at the Union."

"You live in Oxford? I read economics at Worcester College."

"Yes, I know. In actual fact I live in London now. By coincidence I was in Oxford for a meeting at my alma mater, Queen's College. I was intrigued when I heard you were speaking at the Union, so I popped by to hear you. It's not every day I get to listen to the former U.S. of A. Treasury Secretary." She had well rehearsed her answer to the question she had expected.

"I see. You flatter me, Elizabeth."

"I was very impressed by your speech that night. Then I saw the replay of your speech at the World Trade Center on BBC and I wanted to get involved. So I volunteered and, well, here I am."

"So you work in London, then?"

"No, actually my family keeps a flat there. I do a few tasks for the family business. What ever Daddy asks of me."

"Oh?"

"In actual fact, when I told Daddy of my interest in your position on terrorism, he was very enthusiastic about my volunteering."

Mark was seated in the front seat of the modest sized car. They chatted amiably about Oxford and London as she drove. "You're doing very well in driving a left hand drive." Mark observed.

"I rented it at the Logan airport the other day and am somewhat used to it. I have to pay extra careful attention though."

From the beginning Mark saw that Elizabeth was a very attractive woman. It was a pleasant surprise. He had quite expected the campaigning to be rather drab and bleak. This development would ease the pain a bit.

At the Centennial Hotel in Concord, Elizabeth's room was next to Mark's. She waited to telephone England until it was likely that Derek's car was on its way to the London office. "I'm making very good progress," she told Derek. "I'm acting as his driver here in New Hampshire."

"And have you discovered anything worth noting?" Hardin demanded.

"No, I haven't. And I'm not certain what I might discover. It could be nothing. Nothing important at all. But I'm doing what you requested."

"Has he made any advances toward you?"

Elizabeth laughed. "Not unless you call staring at my knees and legs making an advance."

"Goodbye, Elizabeth," Derek ended their conversation with no hint of humor.

As Elizabeth turned out the lamp, she felt uncomfortable. Was her eccentric boss expecting her to have an affair with Stevens? And even if she did what would that accomplish? Anyway she didn't like the whole idea. But, as she pulled up the warm blanket, she thought about the three million pound salary and went to sleep.

But the next morning, as she brushed her hair, she wondered, was she willing to turn herself into a prostitute for three million pounds?

The speech in Concord went was well as could be expected. Mark's point about the threat to American embassies was listened to attentively and the Q & A session was very similar to the others. Mark emphasized his fruitless warnings to the President, but to Mark the absence of Knox made the discussion seem empty. He wished there could be a spirited debate. But Knox was playing it smart. He was the incumbent and obviously felt that a debate would not be to his advantage.

That night, Mark invited Elizabeth to dinner at the Granite Restaurant, an eatery that had been recommended by the hotel desk clerk. She was a delightful companion—intelligent and, of course, pretty, very pretty. They made small talk about their respective experiences at Oxford and how London had changed so much with the influx of foreigners.

"No, London isn't the same as it was when I first knew it," Mark said. He told about his excitement when he and Rodney had first taxied down Piccadilly so many years ago. They laughed about the young Mark's amazement at seeing Queen Elizabeth and Prince Phillip in their stately Rolls-Royce leaving the palace livery.

"I never met the Queen," commented Elizabeth. "But Daddy saw her in person when he was in Parliament and at other events." Mark was curious about his younger companion. "Daddy" was obviously a very successful man.

Mark rode in the front seat next to Elizabeth as they traveled to various New Hampshire towns, where Mark made the same basic speech. He spoke at the small town of Bow, then Londonderry, and the shipyard at Portsmouth. He was getting newspaper coverage in the various towns but only a little television coverage—he hoped the coverage was statewide. Mark was tired as they drove. He would be glad when the campaigning would be over. It had become clear to Mark that the big multi-state primary date in February would have to be conducted largely by television. The candidates could not possibly make extended appearances in each of the many states. Knox had stuck to his decision to not campaign in New Hampshire. Mark thought he was making some headway with the voters. The questions from the audiences seemed to be less confrontational. They were more about the terrorist threat and less about other issues.

It was the Democrats who were getting the real coverage. Their race was wide open and attracting more crowds. Two senators, three governors and a few also-rans were the candidates.

Mark's last speech in New Hampshire was in Bretton Woods. "I've been looking forward to speaking to the Republicans of this famous city." He was not sure that many knew of the Bretton Woods meetings and agreements among the financial leaders of the great powers, just before World War II ended. "You see, when I was studying that earth shaking agreement, I was a student at the University of California. I learned of your town and the momentous plan that tied world currencies to the United States dollar. But that was long ago. The dollar is no longer as important in the world as it was years ago. But the United States is still the most important nation in the world, and that is why this new al Qaeda movement has targeted our country. First it will be our embassies and then God-only knows-what next. Our Capitol building? The White House? Our electricity sources? These people must be stopped and stopped now!"

One of the questions from the listeners gave Mark an opportunity to speak on a subject that had always puzzled him. "How can you justify your stances on abortion, on gays and some of these other things and still claim to be a Republican?"

"I have always thought it a rather mysterious oddity," Mark answered. "You see, Republicans are supposed to believe in freedom of choice of the individual. The government should not dictate to free people. Right?"

"Well—yes," answered the questioner. The man hesitated, perhaps anticipating a trap.

"Well, then, why do conservatives want to outlaw the woman's right to choose? Why do they want to prevent gays from marrying? Isn't this legislating against individual rights? Governmental interference?"

"But wait," said the man."

"Yes, 'but wait,' is correct. Why do the Democrats who seem to want to regulate everything? Heavy taxes on the so-called rich, minimum wage, you name it. Yet they scream bloody murder when others want to regulate the woman's right to choose, gay marriage, you name it. Just ask the A.C.L.U.

"I think it's inconsistent. Even weird," Mark continued. "But I'm not here to answer that question. I'm not even here to get elected President. I'm here to warn the nation about this new terrorist threat. I'm here in your town to wake you up to this threat!"

The audience seemed stunned by his statement that he didn't expect to be President. There was only a smattering of polite applause.

* * *

Mark and Elizabeth dined at the hotel and left the White Mountain city heading back to Manchester, where the plane was waiting for the trip to New York.

Mark had become fond of Elizabeth. She was a delightful companion. She, with her good looks, high heels and short skirt, reminded him of his early feelings for Christina so many years ago.

Their hotel that night provided them a two-bedroom suite with a common living room.

Exhausted as he was, Mark couldn't sleep. He put on his robe and flipped on the TV in the living room. He made himself a Rob Roy—the usual Scotch with some sweet vermouth. He found himself watching an old movie. The main character in the movie explained why he wanted a woman in his life so badly. "Man gave his rib to create woman and has been trying ever since to make himself whole again by having a woman with him," the character explained to his wife. Mark smiled at the truism of the metaphor.

Elizabeth could not sleep either. She heard the television in the next room and realized Mark was awake also. She donned her short nightgown to join him. She went to her door, but hesitated. Was tonight to be the test? Should she make an attempt to seduce Mark? She admired Mark and had become fond of him this past week. He was a brilliant man, a man of conviction and courage Perhaps she would not be prostituting herself in view of her positive feelings toward him. No, she thought, it was not love she felt. She was certain she had never really loved any man, yet she was not a virgin. There would be nothing wrong with making love with a man such as Mark Stevens. A man of power. A man so principled he was running for President even though he had no chance of success. What about this man? Would he respond to her? She knew very well that most men would succumb. She made up her mind and entered the living room.

"May I join you?" she asked.

"Couldn't sleep either?"

"No. This may be our last night together. You're flying to New York after tomorrow's appearance."

"You're not going with me?"

"Depends on what assignment your people give me. Nothing so far."

She sat next to Mark on the small love seat, ignoring the nearby easy chair. She could see him looking closely at her. She could think of little else she could do to entice him. It was up to him to respond. And, even though she had mixed feelings about her situation, she hoped and expected he would respond.

"Would you join me in a drink?" Mark asked.

"Yes, please. A glass of wine would be lovely."

Mark went to the cabinet. "White, I assume."

He handed her the glass and stood by the love seat. He was not stupid, after all. Elizabeth had made her intention clear.

Mark was conflicted. He thought of Christina. Even though they saw each other infrequently, he loved Christina. They had a history together. It was true that their lovemaking was different from what it once was— less passionate—more mature now—deeper, really—a different kind of emotion from that of their early torrid love affair. And more. What about loyalty to Christina? They had made no promises to one another. Yet Mark knew, even feared that if he succumbed to Elizabeth, it would change things with Christina.

Mark took the chair across from Elizabeth. The temptation, while it had not disappeared, had passed. He had made a decision. By not sitting next to Elizabeth, he had sent her a message. There would be no affair—at least not tonight.

CHAPTER SIXTEEN

Elizabeth was sleepless that night.

She had mixed feelings about what had happened. What was her purpose here with Mark's campaign supposed to be? She hadn't learned a thing unusual about Mark's campaign. Certainly nothing that would ruin his campaign. And why had Derek Hardin wanted her to have sex with the man? Was it supposed to be some sort of scandal? Ye Gods! Mark was unmarried. In this age he could sleep with whomever he wanted without repercussions. Maybe Hardin thought if she had a relationship with Mark she could learn some dark secret that existed. What good would that do Hardin anyway? Hardin was unbalanced. Yes, even crazy. She had known that for years. He didn't have to have a rational reason for his actions. And this terrorist venture of his was the craziest of all.

But, more important than all of this, she was relieved. Although she supposed she was willing to have sex with Mark, if he had shown an interest. And, parenthetically, she had to admit, she was surprised that Mark hadn't taken her bait, and to a degree it had bothered her ego not a little. Yet she was relieved at the rejection because she didn't want to turn herself into a whore. That was what it would have amounted to. She would have been a whore. In listening to his speeches she had grown to like Mark. He was brave to take up issues that were controversial. And, although she had personal knowledge that he was absolutely right about the terrorist threat, she could see from the voters' reactions that Mark wasn't convincing most people.

She knew she wouldn't sleep until she called London. She had to tell Hardin that she had failed. That she didn't want the three million. She wanted to come home. Back to her old job.

Mark didn't sleep right away either. Part of him wondered why he had not taken up Elizabeth's not very subtle offer. In years gone by he would not have hesitated. Certainly he loved Christina. But they were not married and they had made no promises. They had not even had time to make love before she left for Rome. Years ago in California it had not bothered his conscience to have sex with Christina even though she was married. Yes, even though he had respect for her then husband, Antonio. Over the years he had had affairs. Several. Perhaps many. None had bothered him. Perhaps his libido had slowed down. But Elizabeth was an attractive woman. Very attractive. And he was lonely. He needed femininity in his life. Yet he had passed up this golden opportunity. Maybe tomorrow he would not pass it up. Yet he knew to the contrary. He thought of Christina. He loved her. He would have had a sense of disloyalty to her. He was on a mission in this campaign. He had to warn the nation.

The last thing he needed was to balance a love affair with the purpose of his campaign. He guessed it was because he was older than he was years ago. Whatever all this conflict was, he was tired, very, very tired. He fell asleep.

"Mr. Hardin, I'm afraid I have to report that I've failed. I've not learned anything of value, even though I've been with him night and day for a week now." Elizabeth had called on her mobile phone.

"I'm sorry to learn that. I had expected more. Much more."

"That's just it! I don't know what you expected me to learn."

"Elizabeth, every man has something to hide. I had expected you to find it."

She was near tears. "As I say, I didn't."

"Did you, how will I say it, turn on your feminine charms? I'm certain you know what I mean."

"I did. Except that last night he refused me."

"Refused you? That's not the Mark Stevens I know."

"I'm afraid it's true." She dabbed her eyes with a tissue. She was afraid of this man, Hardin.

"I want you to come home immediately," Derek ordered.

"Yes, sir."

But Hardin had terminated the call.

"Assad, I have a mission for you." As usual Derek Hardin did not identify himself.

"And what is that?" answered Assad. He was in his office in Tamar, having just awoken in the small bed in the corner.

"I want you to have someone take care of Elizabeth. She's returning from America tomorrow—someplace called New Hampshire."

"And just who is Elizabeth and what do you mean by 'take care of?'"

Derek was angry. He owed this man no explanation. Without his money Assad and his mission would blow up in his ugly unshaven face. "She's one of my employees. A Vice President, if you will. I sent her to spy on Stevens. She's learned nothing. Absolutely nothing of value. She can't even get him into bed."

"She must be an ugly one from what you've told me about Mark Stevens." Assad thought Derek was joking.

But the attempt at humor only further angered Derek. "I want her killed. Killed as soon as possible. She knows too much."

"What do you mean she knows too much. What have you told her?"

Derek's anger totally spilled over. "You idiot! She knows everything."

"You mean about the embassy bombings?" Assad was equally angry and veritably screamed into the phone. "You mean she knows of you and me. Knows you've been supplying the money? You're the one who's an idiot."

Derek didn't answer. Perhaps he knew he had made a serious mistake in the plan to use Elizabeth. Although he would never admit it, even to himself. "Send someone to London immediately. She must be killed as soon as possible."

Assad sat at his desk alone for several minutes, pondering. Then he made up his mind.

First, he called in his chief assistant. "Hussain, I have a little task for you. Mr. Hardin wants you to fly to London. He has an assistant who has learned too much about our operations. She must be disposed of as soon as possible."

"Yes, sir." They spoke in Arabic.

"I want you to report to his offices. Hardin will tell you her name and where she lives. He'll tell you more details. You can get a weapon from our cell leader there in London."

"That won't be necessary, sir."

"It won't?"

"No. I'll just use my hands the way I have on other assignments."

"Very well. I want you to leave tomorrow."

"Yes, sir."

"I'm counting on you."

"Yes, sir."

After Hussain left the room, Assad telephoned his cell leader in Rome.

It had now become clear to Assad. Hardin's order to call off the embassy bombings had only one purpose. Hardin hated Mark Stevens and was waiting for some opportunity to kill Stevens. A murder that would not serve the purpose of Assad and his terrorist plans, but would appeal to Hardin's unbalanced hatred of Stevens. It was Hardin's ego trip and that was all.

"Antonio, this is Assad."

"Yes. I haven't heard from you since the bombing was postponed. My men are very restless." They spoke in broken English.

"Plans have changed. I want you to proceed with the bombing of the embassy."

"That's good news. My men will be very pleased. It will take several days to get them organized."

"Very well. Call me when you're ready. The timing will be important."

"This is very exciting news."

"And one more important thing. Very important."

"And what is that?"

"You are never to say that this order came from Tamar. As far as anyone in the organization is concerned, the immediate destruction of the embassy was strictly your own idea."

"Oh?"

"Yes, your act must be in defiance of the previous order to halt operations. Am I clear about this? Your own idea, not mine."

"Yes. Whatever you say."

"And one other thing. I received intelligence that one of the *Il Verita* reporters has survived and may soon be in Rome."

"I thought he was dead."

"So did we all. But I want him dead. I want you to find him and kill him."

"It will be a pleasure."

Assad knew that Hardin must never find out that he had ordered the Rome bombing in violation of the Englishman's instructions. Without a doubt, Hardin would be very angry to know of Assad's complicity. Anger that could cause the ego-driven man to cut off the much needed funding.

Mark was in his New York apartment. Tomorrow he and Rolf and his newly hired advisors would begin preparation for his TV spot announcements that, at great expense, would pepper the remaining state primaries. He planned to make quick trips for appearances in several of the larger states prior to the February voting. But the main campaigning for the big day would be through TV and appearances on various Internet outlets. His emphasis would be on the terrorist threats, even though the polls showed that likely voters were still unbelieving.

"I would suggest you make some television appearances that will get to the Iowa and New Hampshire voters before they go to the polls. Mario, the *Il Verita* reporter, arrived last night and is sleeping in the other room. We'll use him in the TV spots," said Rolf. "You shouldn't totally write off those two states even though the polls show you'll get less than ten percent of the Republican vote at this point."

"I agree to using Mario," said Mark. "We'll need an Italian translator."

The phone rang. It was Rodney calling from London. "There's an item in the *Times* I thought I should tell you about."

"Really?"

"Let me read it to you."

"Okay."

"Elizabeth Cannon was found dead in her flat this morning. 'She appears to have been strangled' said Chief

Inspector Scott of Scotland Yard. 'We know of no motive for the killing.' The victim was a high-ranking executive of Global Albion of London. A spokesman for her employer, the investment arm of financier Derek Hardin stated that he was shocked at the news. Elizabeth was a valued executive and we are all saddened. Hardin was at his estate in Sussex and had not appeared at the office. He was, no doubt, in mourning,' said the spokesman.'"

"Wow!" exclaimed Mark. "That must be the same Elizabeth who has been driving me around New Hampshire. I'm certain her name was Cannon. She fed me a bunch of bullshit about her background. Evidently her so-called father was not her father at all, but was Derek Hardin all the time.

"Really. I had no idea. I just thought you'd be interested in Derek's making the newspaper."

"What has Derek to do with my campaign? I smell a rat someplace, but I'll be damned if I know what it is."

"I don't know either, but you can bloody well know he's after you in some way."

"Rodney, see what you can find out about his firm, Albion something?"

"Global Albion?"

"Yes, that's it. Hire a private investigator, if you think it wise. Derek was at my speech at the Oxford Union. I wondered why he was there. Why would he have cared about my speech? I'm sure he's up to something. We'd better find out."

The two talked a bit about the hotel investment negotiations and then were saying goodbye. "We've got to find out about Derek. Do what you can, my friend," concluded Mark.

When Mark, with Mario, returned to the apartment that night after filming several TV spots in midtown, there was a blinking light on his telephone. He was tired and poured himself a drink before calling the concierge. Mario, still not accustomed to the time change, went to his room. He intended to return to Rome in the morning. Mark sat, sipping his drink and listening to music. He was generally satisfied with today's work. He had briefly introduced Mario, who told, through the interpreter, about the terrorist training facility in Tamar, the bombing plot of the Rome United States embassy, his narrow escape from Tamar and the murder of his fellow reporter. The other TV spots focused on the terrorist threat and the indifference of President Knox. He had repeatedly made clear that his purpose in running for office was not to become President, but to awaken the nation. The spots were to be telecast in both Iowa and New Hampshire. The elections were very soon now. Mark made a second Rob Roy and answered the blinking light.

"Sir, there is a message from a Rodney Ashley in London, who wants you to telephone him. He says you have the number."

Mark was excited. Perhaps Rodney had found something about Derek's involvement. "Rodney, what's going on? Have you been able to retain an investigator?"

"No, not yet. But that's not why I telephoned."

"Oh, what then?"

"You'll never believe this. There's been another murder. Let me read from the newspaper."

Mark took a sip of his drink and listened.

"It's in the *Times*. 'The body of Robert Marsden was found at his home last night. Marsden had just returned from New York, apparently on business for his employer, Global Albion. Marsden had been strangled. Global Albion is an international banking firm owned and controlled by Derek Hardin. Scotland Yard is investigating the relationship, if any, between the Marsden murder and the very recent murder of another high-ranking official of Global Albion, Elizabeth Cannon. No one at Global Albion could be reached for comment.'"

"My God, what's going on?" Mark exclaimed.

"You don't suppose Derek is involved?" asked Rodney.

"Murdering his own people. I wouldn't put it past him, but I don't see what his motive could be."

"It could be, pure jealousy."

"What do you mean," Mark asked. "Jealousy? Jealous of what?"

"That Cannon woman was working in your campaign, wasn't she?"

"Yes, but—"

"All I know is that it would be just like Derek Hardin to try to stop you from being President."

"But I don't want to be President. I'm just trying to wake up the country—"

"To the terrorist threat, I know. But Derek doesn't know that."

"Well, you'd better drop your work on the hotel deal and get the best investigator you can find. We've got to find out what the hell is going on!"

"Right you are."

The next morning, Mario was having a quick breakfast before going to Kennedy Airport and back to Rome. Mark asked the Italian American chef from the kitchen to come to the apartment to act as an interpreter. Mark wanted to tell Mario about the murders.

"Mario sees no connection," said the chef. "But he had heard that a wealthy Englishman had flown to Tamar for a meeting with Assad. He remembered that he had seen the Englishman get on his plane and that he was very well dressed, considering how hot it was in Tamar," said the interpreter.

Mark bid Mario *ciao* and thanked him for doing the television ads. He pondered the recent events, but no connection to Derek occurred to him.

CHAPTER SEVENTEEN

It was an interesting night when the Iowa caucus returns came in. Mark and Rolf watched the returns on television in the New York apartment. Mark had not expected that he would get many votes, despite the TV ad with Mario telling the listeners that the terrorist threat was very real. The ad had not hit Iowa television until the Sunday before the caucuses on this Tuesday. Nevertheless, he hoped he'd have a decent showing.

Before many of the Republican returns came in, the network pundits reported the exit polls. A fair number of the interviews showed that the voters had taken the terrorist threat warnings seriously. But that did not necessarily translate into votes for Mark, the exit polls showed. Mark's run for the nomination was receiving national press coverage. It had been many years since a serious challenge had been made against a sitting President in the nomination process. About 11:00 in the evening the trend had become clear. Mark had garnered 11 percent of the Iowa delegates to Knox's 89 percent.

"Yes, I'm disappointed," Mark told Rolf, "But at least I convinced 11 percent. Maybe, at least, I got the other 89 percent to do some thinking."

"The important person to get to do some serious thinking is Stuart Knox." Rolf retorted.

"Yeah, he'll get the nomination all right. I don't have a chance to beat him. But maybe now he'll pay more attention to what I've been telling him this past year."

"You know, Iowans are very conservative people. Maybe some of your other positions—on the abortion amendment—on banning gay marriages—turned them off."

"Probably, but I had to tell them the truth."

The next morning, Mark made a decision.

"Rolf, I'm flying to New Hampshire this afternoon. I want to show the voters in person that I care how they vote."

This time Mark drove himself to the various New Hampshire towns, mostly making appearances to small groups. This trip there was no pretty English woman to be his driver. He remained puzzled by Elizabeth's murder and the mysterious fact that she worked for Derek, but he needed to concentrate on the campaign.

When the campaigning was finished, Mark called Rolf in New York, "I've decided to stay in Manchester on election night and then fly back to San Francisco to decide exactly what to do."

"Good," responded Rolf. "I'd like to go home for a while my self."

"Tomorrow I'll fly down to New York and pick you up."

"Good luck on the election returns. I'll be glued to the television."

Mark switched from one channel to another as the returns came in. He wanted to hear the different reporters opinions and prognostications.

Finally it was nearly over. Ninety percent of the votes in the Republican primary were counted. "President Stuart Knox has won 72 percent and Mark Stevens a surprising 28 percent," said the CNN anchor.

"What does this mean?" asked the co-anchor.

"Perhaps his message is getting through. That this terrorist revival is real, even imminent."

"And that he has warned the President repeatedly and nothing is being done."

"Yet, it appears that Knox is a shoo-in to retain the Republican nomination."

"Yes, Knox's real problem is going to be the Democratic candidate, after the Democrats decide who that'll be."

"And who that will be is not at all certain as yet."

Mark flipped off the television and went to bed.

He'd fly to San Francisco with Rolf tomorrow, but, as sleep neared, he yearned to be with Christina. He wanted to hold her, talk with her, yes, and to make love with her.

It was the next day in the New York apartment. "Rolf, I've decided I need to go to Rome, and not San Francisco. Only for a few days. Then I'll be back campaigning."

"I understand. That's fine with me."

"I'll charter a jet to take you home."

"No way. I'll grab a commercial flight and be out of here today. Enjoy your stay with Christina. You need a break, my old friend." Rolf fully understood Mark's need to be with Christina. He knew his friend's love for her. Passion he had seen in Mark since they had been seniors at Cal-Berkeley, so many years ago. In fact he wished he could have such feelings for a woman. Even when he had first married, he never had felt the same emotion. And now, so many years after his own divorce, he had given up hope.

Exhausted, Mark had slept most of the way on the flight to Rome. As was her custom, Christina drove him to her villa outside Rome in her old, perfectly maintained, red Ferrari convertible. Although the weather was cold, she had the top down and her long blonde hair flowed in the wind, as it had the first time she had driven him in the now vintage car.

It was the middle of the night and the first thing they each wanted to do was to make love. They needed each other right then.

Talking could wait until tomorrow. Mark was glad he had not succumbed to the temptation of his New Hampshire aide.

The next morning at breakfast they brought each other up to date. Mark wore the bathrobe he kept at her villa. Christina wore a white robe made of lace. "Do you think you have a chance at getting the nomination?" As always, her accent was more pronounced when she was out of practice speaking English.

"Frankly, I'm still pretty certain I don't want the nomination. My goal is still to wake up the country. Besides, I don't have a chance to beat Knox. He knows he's got the nomination in his pocket. I predict he'll not do much campaigning for the big primaries coming up."

Mark told Christina about the murdering of the two top aides of Derek Hardin. "It's a mystery to me. This Margaret Cannon was a volunteer driver in my campaign in New Hampshire. She told me a bunch of lies about her background. Now I find out she worked for Derek."

"Strange," Christina commented.

"So strange, that I've asked Rodney to hire an investigator to look into this Global Albion Limited, Derek's company in London."

"Wait. I have an idea. *Il Verita* has an investigative reporter in London. Would you like him to see what he can find out?"

"Good idea. Thanks. Put him on it, if you care to."

"I'll call him this afternoon."

"Christina! Signorena Christina!" The maid was obviously very excited, but Mark couldn't understand what she was saying.

"She wants me to turn on the television. Quickly. Something has happened."

They quickly walked to another room where Christina turned on the TV.

Mark couldn't understand what the announcer was saying, but the picture showed a large building in smoldering ruins.

"They've bombed the American Embassy!" Christina shouted. Just look! It's Via Vittoria Veneto! My God they've done it!"

"I can't believe it," Mark shouted. They really went ahead and did it! How did they ever get in it with all the guards and barriers!'

" Quiet. Let's listen."

The announcer was speaking excitedly in Italian.

"The police have no idea how they got inside. The loss of life seems very high," reported Christina.

"Christina. Let's drive down there right now!"

The police had Via Vittoria Veneto, with its stately trees, blocked off. Christina showed her newspaper credentials to the officer in charge and drove her Mercedes into the devastated area. The scene was chaos. The front of the embassy was in shambles. They left the car and made their way through the ambulances and television trucks. Bloody victims of the blast were being loaded into the ambulances. Many bodies lay on the street as yet uncovered. The coroner's vehicles had not yet arrived. Some tattered survivors were walking about in a dazed condition. Policemen were attempting to interview the more coherent ones. No one seemed to have any idea as to how the bombers had succeeded in their terrible deed, despite the security measures. Mark wondered if they had somehow planted their devilish devices during the night.

So, Mario had been right. Mark had been right in his attempts to warn the United States government and its people. Damned Knox! He had persistently warned President Knox, but to no avail. The man did not deserve re-election. Mark had to get home and campaign more vigorously than he had planned.

"Christina, dear. I've got to get the hell out of here. I've got to return home. Who knows what these terrorists plan to do next. I had planned on spending more time with you, but events always seem to stand in our way."

Christina had tears in her eyes. "I understand. I'll drive you to your plane.

Mark was steely-eyed. It was a time for action, not tears.

On the flight home Mark talked to Rodney. "Yes, Sky News is talking about little else besides the Rome bombing. It's horrible."

"Horrible is a mild word. Absolute devastation. I'm on my way to San Francisco."

"What are your plans?"

"I've made up my mind. I'm going all out for the Presidency. That damned Knox doesn't deserve to be in the White House. And the Democratic candidate, whomever it turns out to be, won't do any better. They were all asleep at the switch too. Besides, the Dems would ruin the economy."

"I'm stunned. What can I do to help?"

"Have you talked to an investigator about this Derek business?"

"I have an appointment tomorrow."

"Good. *Il Verita* has put their best man in London on the Derek angle. Something's going on."

"And you can wager that whatever the connection, it's evil incarnate."

"I can see Greenland out the window now. We're stopping in New York for fuel. I'm going to take on board some of my campaign people. We've got to work out a winning strategy—and do it fast."

Mark hadn't felt such enthusiasm since he resigned as Secretary of the Treasury. Its just too damn bad that it took that disaster in Rome to do it, he thought.

Derek called Assad from his car on his way into London.

"What in God's name are you doing? I gave a strict order that there should be no attack on the Rome embassy and now this!"

"I just heard about the embassy bombing less than 15 minutes ago. I personally told our leader in Rome to hold off. He has defied my direct order. I shall have him eliminated as soon as possible."

"You have my permission to kill him. Perhaps that will teach others they have to obey orders."

Assad grinned. He had no intention of eliminating his man in Rome, especially after such a magnificent performance. He'd simply tell Hardin that the deed was done and have his man lie low for a while. Hardin would never know the difference. "Yes, sir. It will be done," Assad lied.

"This may ruin my whole scheme," Derek responded. "This could get Stevens elected. Damn! Assad you've really, as the Americans would say, screwed up."

"I'm sorry, but it wasn't my fault."

But the phone was dead. Derek had hung up.

Rolf came down from Sonoma to Mark's Nob Hill condominium to meet with Mark and his small group of paid political advisors. They decided to double the number of TV ads, emphasizing the embassy bombing and using clips of Mark's speeches warning of the terrorist threats. Mark would make as many speeches as possible, particularly in the large states starting with California. The invitations to appear on the Sunday TV shows, as well as other talk shows, were pouring in. That was a good way to reach the voters nationwide. But it was also necessary to press as much flesh as possible. If he were to win the Presidency, it was mandatory that the people like him. He needed to show his human side.

CHAPTER EIGHTEEN

He hopped the cable car down Nob Hill to San Francisco's Union Square for his first rally in his nationwide push. Mark made his way through the crowded car—introducing himself and shaking hands. Many were tourists from all over the globe. "How do you do? I'm Mark Stevens. I'm running for President." He had mixed feelings about what he was doing. He was glad to meet the people, yet he felt like just another pandering politician.

There had been little advance publicity, so the crowd in the square was small. Besides, the clear majority of San Francisco voters were Democrats and not likely to be interested in the Republican primary. But Mark made the best of it. He spoke from the center of the square and made the same basic speech that he had made so many times in Iowa and New Hampshire. But since then there had been the bombing in Rome.

"While I was still in the cabinet I warned President Knox repeatedly of the terrorists' plot to bomb the American embassy in Rome. My warnings were ignored. 'Everything is under control. There is no threat. You are a scaremonger,' was all Knox told me. Now look what has happened. Dozens of Americans have been murdered. All due to Knox's inaction. Actually all of America's inaction. The whole world has been asleep these past years. My purpose in running was to awaken the government. To awaken the public that the struggle against terrorism is not over!"

"But what about the other issues?" a voice from the crowd demanded. "What about the right of gays to marry?"

"I've consistently said that I am not opposed to gay marriage. The institution of marriage is more threatened by the divorce rate than it is by gay marriage!" There was a smattering of applause. "But I'm telling, you this new terrorist activity is far more important than any other issue facing the American public."

"You've been saying that you don't really want to be President. But now you seem have changed your mind. Why?" asked another in the small crowd.

Mark was keenly aware of the television cameras. What he said would in all likelihood be on tonight's news "True," Mark continued. "But I realize, since the bombing in Rome, that I would be better able to respond to this threat than President Knox and certainly better than any of the Democrats seeking their nomination."

"What would you do as President?" asked the questioner. "Get us into another Iraq war?"

"Mark knew that most San Franciscans had been opposed to the Iraq war from its very beginning.

"Whether I'd actually invade Tamar or not is not evident yet. But I would certainly put pressure on the King to rid his tiny island of this new al Qaeda."

"But would you invade, if pressure didn't work?"

"Absolutely, I would. Who knows where they would bomb next? The White House? The Capitol?"

There were several boos from the group as Mark headed for his vintage Rolls that stood waiting near the corner. Jorge had loaded Mark's luggage into the big trunk. "Let's go to the airport, before they ask any more questions. I don't think this went over very well." Mark was going to fly to Los Angeles where he would make more television ads and speak before L.A.'s Town Hall and the World Affairs Council. He needed to refine his message. Make it more effective. After L.A., he would fly to Washington, D.C., where he was to record appearances for the Sunday network talk shows.

As he stepped off his plane at Washington D.C.'s Ronald Reagan Airport, some of the press approached him. Several television cameras were at the scene.

"Mr. Stevens," one member of the press said. "Have you heard about Premier Assad's blog on his website?"

"No, I haven't. More threats?"

"No, just the opposite."

"The opposite?"

"Assad denied responsibility for the embassy bombing. He said it must have been some rogue operation. In any event, it had nothing to do with him or Tamar. Do you have any comment, sir?"

For a long moment Mark was taken aback by the news. But answered, "I don't believe Assad! Not for one minute. He's been planning this operation for months, perhaps years. We need to be all the more alert."

Mark took the back seat of the waiting S.U.V. He had to think. What was the best way to handle this unexpected ploy? He was certain that it would come up in the interviews for the Sunday shows.

To Mark's surprise, President Knox was to be given the first 15 minutes of the interviews on the first network show. Mark would follow with his 15 minutes.

Mark sat in the so-called green room, watching the interview with Knox on the monitor.

"Mr. President, what do you say to the Internet announcement by General Assad that he was not responsible for the bombing of our embassy in Rome?"

"I think it shows conclusively that former Secretary Stevens was incorrect in his many statements that the little kingdom of Tamar was going to strike against our embassy. I have always been assured by our intelligence agencies that Tamar was not reviving the al Qaeda threat. And I repeatedly told Stevens that he was wrong. That's why I asked him to resign his post in my cabinet."

"But, sir, we all know now that there was some sort of plot to destroy the embassy. What do you intend to do?"

"Obviously, there are some terrorists in the world. There will always be some screwballs. We will root them out and they will be punished. Severely punished. But al Qaeda has long been destroyed. I can assure the American people of that fact."

Mark was livid with anger. Knox was simply taking Assad at his word. The word of a maniac who was not to be believed. The word of a man who killed an *Il Verita* reporter who was trying to warn the world what was going on. And now telling the outright lie in claiming he had asked Mark to resign from the cabinet.

Finally it was Mark's turn to be interviewed.

"Secretary Stevens, you were in the green room and saw my interview with the President?"

"Yes, I was. First of all, President Knox is lying about asking me to resign. Despite our disagreement over the terrorist threat, he wanted me to stay on at least until he was re-elected. He wanted to use my name to show that he had a strong financial team. I resigned anyway."

"What about the President's view about Assad? What is your view about Assad's denial of any role in the Rome bombing?"

"Taking the word of a known terrorist! I am appalled. I have presented evidence that Assad is operating an extensive terrorist training camp on Tamar. If the C.I.A. had its act together they would know about that. The bombing was not done by some independent rogue group. Assad's denial is just part of his strategy until the next act of terrorism."

The rest of the 15 minutes were spent on Mark's positions on various domestic issues that had been brought up in the campaigns in Iowa and New Hampshire.

"Finally, Secretary Stevens. When you first announced your candidacy for President, you repeatedly said that you were not actually trying to be President, but were only trying to warn the nation of the threat. Why have you changed your mind? Indeed, you actually have changed your mind, haven't you?"

"I am reminded of the late William F. Buckley's answer to a questioner when Buckley ran for mayor of

New York, years ago. 'What if you were actually elected?' he was asked. I would demand a recount,' Buckley said. At first I felt the way Buckley felt. I didn't want to be President. I just wanted to make a point. A very serious point that President Knox had ignored.

"But, as I said recently in San Francisco, when the bombing in Rome occurred, I realized that Stuart Knox was incapable of facing the truth. I could see that I was able to respond to the threat and that President Knox was frozen in his old belief. And I might add that I would be far better able than any of the crop running for the Democratic nomination."

"What makes you think so?"

"Listen, I served with Stuart Knox. I know him well. He's just a good politician who knows how to get elected. But his whole purpose in life is to get himself re-elected for a second term. That does not make for good government. As for the Democrats, well there is little difference between their leading candidates and Knox. They all want power. All they want to do with that power is to get themselves to stay in power. Haven't we had enough of that sort of governing?"

"Do you really expect to get the Republican nomination away from a sitting President?"

"I admit that the chances are slim. My task in the few remaining days before the voting, on the first Tuesday in February, is to get my message across to the voters. I intend to do as much campaigning as possible and to win the nomination in Los Angeles."

"Would you consider running on a third party ticket?"

"I intend to win at the convention. I intend to be the Republican nominee. After the convention, you can ask Stuart Knox if he intends to form a third party."

The next week the polls showed Mark had made some headway, but he was still woefully behind Knox. He had still to get his message out, that al Qaeda was a serious threat.

CHAPTER NINETEEN

Derek's plane landed at Tamar. As Derek stepped onto the tarmac, Assad offered a profuse apology to his angry supporter: "I cannot possibly control everyone of these cells across the world. You can't expect me to."

Derek said nothing as they walked into Assad's humble office near the airport. Both men were seated and Derek began. "I hold you totally responsible! I wouldn't put it past you to have given your go ahead with the bombing. Do you realize what you have done? You fool!"

Assad didn't know what to say to this eccentric man who controlled the supply of money for his operation. He didn't relish this abuse, but what was he to do? "The men in Rome will be disciplined," he meekly said. Assad felt as if he were a bullfighter with the just-released bull charging after him. He had to be adroit, at least for now.

"Disciplined! Is that all you can say? I want them eliminated!" Derek stood defiantly, shaking his finger at his fellow conspirator. "Do you hear me? Eliminated! The same as you had my employees. Eliminated."

"But they are valuable men."

"Do you know the meaning of the word eliminated? Killed!

I want them killed before the week is out!"

Assad was torn. He had to think of some way to save his men and yet make it so that this maniac thought his orders had been followed. "Yes, sir. It will be done, if I have to do it myself. I'll have to find them. They are in hiding. Perhaps in Sicily. I don't know."

Derek went on, raving. "You probably have gotten Mark Stevens elected President of the United States. He'll be a man difficult to deal with."

"I'm sorry, Mr. Hardin. I'm sure the men in Rome didn't understand—"

Derek resumed his seat. "There is only one recourse, left." He was calmer now.

"What is that, Mr. Hardin?" Assad asked.

"It's clear to me. We must see to it that Stevens never takes office."

"And what do you suggest?"

"We kill Stevens. That is what must be done."

Assad did not respond. This man was more of a terrorist than Assad was.

"I'm getting back on my plane and returning to London, immediately. I intend to devise a plan to end the life of this man who has been my nemesis for so many years. I'll give you orders when I have worked it out. In the meantime, I want those responsible for the bombing to be killed. Do you understand?" Derek quickly walked back to his plane. It had been refueled and was ready for the long trip back to England.

Assad sat at his desk. For the first time that he could remember, his hands were shaking. He had dodged the charging bull, at least for now.

It was a few days later. Christina telephoned Mark who was in his hotel in Chicago. He had spent a busy day making campaign appearances in the Windy City. It was only another week until the big first Tuesday in February.

"Mark, dear, my reporter in London has just called me with news about Derek Hardin."

An exhausted Mark had just gone to bed at his North Michigan Avenue hotel. "What is it? What did he find out?"

"Derek Hardin flew to Tamar. He evidently stayed only a short time and then returned to London. He's not in his office. Probably at his country estate."

"How do you know?"

"My reporter saw the flight plan. I told you he was good".

"My God, Christina! Do you know what this means?"

"Derek has some connection to this terrorist business," Christina said.

"I'll bet he's behind the whole affair. I can't believe it! Keep your man on it."

"Another thing," she said. "The police think the bombers had planted the bomb in the embassy months ago. They must have detonated it by remote control."

"My God! I wonder how they got it inside in the first place?" Mark paused before saying goodbye. "Christina, is there any way you could come and be with me? Maybe for just a couple of days. I'm so tired. So very tired of all this."

Christina was swamped with her work on the newspaper. "I'll leave at once. Where? What city?"

"New York. At the apartment."

"I'll meet you there tomorrow."

"Thanks. Thanks more than you know." Mark was asleep in less than a minute.

Christina was at Mark's side as the newly assigned Secret Service took them downtown to the rebuilt World Trade Center. They had made love that morning. Her very presence and support had rejuvenated him. She planned to return to Italy the next morning. Mark's next campaign stop was in Philadelphia and then on to Pittsburgh, followed by Miami. He wished they had more time, but he had learned to be grateful for their few times together. Instead of being overwhelmed by the daunting schedule ahead, he now felt eager. Thanks to Christina.

Mark was nervous. This was the most important speech of his life. The embassy bombing had focused new media attention on him. From reports, a large crowd was expected. He remembered his first speech at the World Trade Center, in what in reality, was several weeks ago, but seemed like years. From only trying to warn the nation of the new terrorist threat, he was now a full-fledged candidate for President of the United States.

"I haven't prepared as much as I would like," he told Christina.

"Why don't you just speak like an Italian?"

"An Italian? What do mean, speak like an Italian?"

"Let your emotional side speak out. Your heart. The emotional Mark that I know so well. The side I fell in love with." Smiling, she squeezed his hand.

"Maybe you're right. But I don't know where to start."

"Just start. And see what happens. They'll love it."

Mark stood at the microphone, the September 11th memorial was surrounded by the tall new buildings. The crowd was much larger than he had ever seen. Where to begin? "*Speak from the heart.*" Christina's words went through his mind. "*Speak from the heart!*" He had no notes. He would ignore the teleprompter.

"My fellow voters. My fellow Americans." It seemed a mundane way to begin, yet that was what had come from his mouth. "I am not a traditional Republican and I am certainly not a Democrat. I am simply me—Mark Stevens. My political advisors have told me that some of my ideas will turn off many of you, perhaps even most of you. But in the words of the old song, 'I gotta be me. I gotta be me.' I am not a politician and I can't follow the advice of political people." As he spoke, he was aware he was using more gestures than customary for him. The crowd was quiet at first, but then broke into applause. Perhaps they were more offended by the typical politicians than they would be by some of the beliefs he would soon present. But Mark didn't care. He was going to tell them what he thought and to hell with the consequences.

"As many of you know, the most important reason I want the Republican nomination is to combat the new terrorism that threatens us—that has already resulted in

173

the destruction of our embassy in Rome. I believe I am
the best qualified to deal with this threat and I will tell
you why before I finish. But I am no longer a single-issue
candidate. The press is asking what my stand is on other
issues and I am certain that many of you are asking the
same question. Well, here goes.

"The issue that still is very important to many
conservatives is the issue of right-to-life. In plain words
the right of a woman to have an abortion. Or, as others
put it, the right of a woman to control her own body.
The issue is not as crystal clear as many would have it.
There are good arguments on both sides. But I'll tell
you what I think. I have to go back. Where does this
right to choose come from? It isn't in the constitution—
certainly not expressly nor, I believe, not implicit. No,
the claimed right comes, not from the constitution, but
from the majority of U.S Supreme Court judges years
ago who hated the idea of some states banning abortion.
Well, I hate the idea of a small group of judges telling the
states they have no power to legislate on the matter—any
matter—unless the constitution forbids the states from
acting. In my opinion the Supreme Court majority in
Roe v. Wade twisted the Constitution to meet with their
own prejudices. And banned the states from acting. Does
this mean I am opposed to abortion? No, it does not
mean that at all. If I were a state legislator, I would not
ban abortion. I would argue that a woman had a right to
choose—a right to control her own body. Think of the
consequences of some states banning abortions and others
not. Women would merely go to another state. As they
used to go to other states to get divorces. An intolerable
situation! That is how I feel. I simply disagree with many

of my fellow conservatives. I think the Republican Party makes a serious mistake in making this the issue of the century. Conservatives believe in free choice, in free markets, in the freedom to conduct one's own affairs. Why do so many believe in taking this freedom away from women? I simply don't understand it."

The crowd was quiet. At first apparently not knowing whether to boo or applaud. But, this after all, was New York City. Finally most of the listeners applauded. "Republicans should drop this divisive issue and get on with it!"

"What about the right of gays to marry. Who cares? Why divide our party over such a stupid issue? If they want to call themselves married, why is it any of my business? As I have said at the beginning of this campaign, more harm is caused to the institution of marriage by divorce than by gay marriage. Clearly, all the gay community is trying to do is to have the rest of us accept them as human beings. Gay people can love and commit to one another the same as the rest of us. For heaven's sake, stop making this into an earth-shaking divisive issue. "What about free trade? Those against free trade, against a worldwide economy, totally ignore the benefits to the largest group affected. The consumer. If one nation's people can make a product cheaper than our own, then it is the U.S. consumer who benefits from lower prices. Sheer competition will drive prices down. Sure, we should help displaced persons learn how to get decent jobs in the global economy, but by training and education, not by trade barriers.

"Some have asked about my relationship with Christina Bagliani. Do I intend to marry Christina? Would I have her live in the White House if I were elected? Is that really any of your business? I love this woman dearly. And have for many years. I have reason to believe she loves me. She has flown from Italy to spend one day with me and to be on this platform with me. But do I intend to marry her? For God's sake, I haven't even asked her. I haven't the slightest idea whether she would accept such a request. Christina Bagliani owns and runs a highly respected international newspaper. She lives in Italy. Would the electorate really expect her to give up her career to be our First Lady? Millions of couples have separate careers. Many thousands of them live far apart. People, this is a new era we all live in! Get with it." The crowd gave an unexpected hearty round of applause. "Ladies and Gentlemen, I would like to introduce you to the love of my life, Christina Bagliani." Mark pointed to Christina. "Please rise, Christina."

Christina stood, smiling. She glowed, with her blond hair more than half way down her back. Again the crowd gave a roar.

"*Speak from the heart.*" Those words of Christina stuck in Mark's mind. She had been right. He felt the crowd was with him.

"There are many other issues that I will shortly address on my website and which will come up as I campaign across the country. But all these issues pale in comparison to the main reason I'm running for President. Terrorism!" Mark paused dramatically and looked from side to side across the crowded memorial site—a crowd whose very size encouraged him to speak like an Italian.

"While I was Secretary of Treasury I warned President Knox—repeatedly warned him—that terrorists intended to destroy the United States Embassy in Rome. The source

of my information, I told him, was Christina Bagliani."
Mark pointed at Christina who gently nodded.

"I told the President that Ms. Bagliani owned the worldwide and reliable newspaper, *Il Verita. Il Verita*, I assured the President, had two investigative reporters who had infiltrated this new al Qaeda organization on the island nation of Tamar. The President ignored my many warnings. 'Nonsense', he said. 'We hadn't had an attack in many years. The government agencies knew of no such threat.' That was all there was to it. After I resigned from the cabinet, I met in Rome with these two brave reporters. They knew what they were talking about. Again, I called the President and warned him. Warned him to no avail! General Assad tried to murder the reporters when they retuned to Tamar. One escaped. His name is Mario. Mario appeared with me here at this very place a few weeks ago and verified the facts. Despite all this, Knox took no action. Then, as you know, the embassy was destroyed, killing hundreds of Americans. What was Knox's response? 'Don't worry, Americans, this was an act of rogue terrorists. Assad has denied any involvement, he assured us. We are taking care of the matter.'"

Many in the audience evidently did not know of these facts for they seemed stunned. There was no applause, no reaction.

Mark left the lectern. The mike attached to his lapel would have to do. "I'm here to tell you we are *not* taking care of the matter. I don't know when the next attack will occur, but be assured there will be another attack. Whether it will be here again at the World Trade Center or the Capitol building or the White House, I do not know. But it *will* occur. Maybe not until after the election in November when the terrorists and their supporters expect Stuart Knox, the sleepy, complacent Stuart Knox, to remain in power. But I'm telling you that it will happen.

"I'm here to make the point you that we have to do something and to do it now. As President, I will act. I urge you, with my very soul to elect me as your President. With your votes, we will win at the convention in Los Angeles and I will defeat the Democratic nominee in November. Americans, it is time to wake up to this threat and we must do it now!"

Finally the crowd reacted with applause. Not as vigorous as Mark would have liked, but at least they reacted.

With the Secret Service in tow, Mark and Christina took the elevators to the top of the new World Trade Center building, where the chartered helicopter was waiting. It would whisk Christina to her jet, up the Hudson to New York's new airport for private planes.

The wind whipped their clothing on top of the tall building. "I was disappointed in the crowd's reaction," Mark told her. "Maybe I'm pulling a Don Quixote, tilting at windmills."

"No, you're not. You simply gave them something to think about. As I understand America's politics you took some unconventional views for a Republican. How do you say it? Maybe they need some time to chew on it."

"I hope you're right. I've got to wake them up. That's what this is all about, even if they disagree with me about other things. People seem to have forgotten that it was near this very spot that September 11 occurred. It's practically a whole new generation."

The helicopter's noisy rotors started up. "Anyway, I can't thank you enough for coming over to see me. It did me more good than you can imagine."

"I wish that I could stay longer. Keep in touch by phone and good luck." Mark pulled her close and kissed her. "Sometimes I think I'm crazy doing all this. We could be on an island someplace in the Mediterranean and away from all these threats."

"Yes, but that wouldn't be you. Mark Stevens sitting in the sun on the lawn of his villa? Never! Goodbye my darling."

Mark watched her helicopter make its way above the Manhattan buildings and disappear. What would happen to their relationship if, by some weird chance, by some fluke, he were elected President and lived in the White House?

As he retuned to the Secret Service S.U.V., he planned to watch television to see what the pundits thought of his speech. Tomorrow he would begin his high-pressure trip across the nation. He wanted to be at home on Nob Hill on the big primary night. Then his quest would be all over. Or would it?

CHAPTER TWENTY

It had been a hectic ten days. Rallies in Philadelphia, Pittsburg, Miami, Atlanta, Chicago Houston, Dallas, Los Angeles, all before returning to San Francisco for a last rally on the day of the nationwide primary voting. Mark had also appeared a final time on the Sunday talk shows. He had made numerous television and Internet ads. No matter the cost, the nation had been saturated with his positions on various matters. He had tried to carefully explain that the main issue was terrorism and had urged the voters to not be distracted by the other issues. Knox's tepid response to the Rome bombing had disgusted Mark and he had made that clear in all his ads and appearances.

Mark was numb. It seemed as if he had been repeating the same speech over and over again. He had grasped so many hands that they all seemed the same. He was exhausted, absolutely exhausted, both physically and mentally. Rolf had come down from Sonoma to Nob Hill to watch the election returns on television with Mark. The contest no longer seemed to be exciting to Mark. He was so very tired. The voting returns were out of his hands. His financial people told him that he had spent maybe $250 million of his own money. He would have to liquidate some of his assets when all the bills came in. But he hardly cared. He had done what he had to do. It was in now in the hands of the Republican, independent, and crossover voters.

Jorge fetched Mark a Rob Roy. Rolf asked for a beer as he flipped on the television.

"The exit polls in New York show it's too close to call," said the Fox News anchor. Pennsylvania showed Knox leading, but by only five points. "My God, Mark," said Rolf. "I think you have a chance." Mark didn't respond. He was just glad it was all over.

The news anchor continued. "As to the Democratic race, it appears that John Morgan has a substantial lead in the early returns."

Rolf switched to public television: "As the night wears on it is becoming clear that the Republican race will not decided until the votes of the Western states are in. We're in for a long night," Rolf repeatedly switched from one channel to the next. Fighting to stay awake on such an important night, Mark had dozed off from time to time. Jorge brought a pot of hot coffee. Mark needed a booster. Win or lose, and surely he would lose, he would have to make a statement before the television cameras. Part of him returned to his former state of mind before he wasn't running to win, but only to make the point about terrorism. And surely he had made the point. But another part had really hoped he might win.

It was ten o'clock. Sufficient returns were in. The networks had made their calls. Some 42% of the

Republican voters had voted for Mark with the 58% staying with Stuart Knox. The delegate count for the convention was about the same.

It was early morning in Italy. Christina would be having her breakfast when Mark telephoned. "Christina dear, the election is over. They have selected Knox."

"I'm sorry, darling."

He gave her the totals.

"What are you going to do next?"

"All I know is that I'm tired. I gave it my best shot. What else is there?"

"The convention. Are you sure you're going to lose at the convention?"

"Oh, yes, without a doubt. Knox has a majority of the delegates.

"I probably won't even make an appearance before the convention."

"You sound dispirited."

"Probably because I am."

"Will Knox win in November?"

"Oh yes. The Democrats have chosen their man. With the economy booming and even the Republicans not believing me about terrorism, Knox is a shoo-in."

"You need some rest. There's been an important development about Derek Hardin, but you go to bed. I'll call you later, when you're not so tired."

Mark felt a surge of energy. "What about Derek?"

"Derek has fled the country with much of his assets. He has gone to Tamar."

"What? Fled the country?"

"Yes, Rodney, being a Lord and all, got the government, Whitehall, to investigate Hardin. They found he was financing Assad. They were going to prosecute him for aiding a terrorist regime. That's why he fled the country."

"My God, I couldn't convince the voters, and yet Rodney, bless him, got something done!" Mark paused. "Derek in Tamar! I don't believe it. So that is what he's been up to! My God!"

"What will you do now?" Christina asked.

"I don't know. I can't think of anything I can do. Except maybe persuade Knox. But there have been no further attacks. I just don't know. I just don't know."

CHAPTER TWENTY-ONE

With all the primary voting completed by early February, the Republicans had moved up their convention in Los Angeles until March. It was a foregone conclusion that Knox would be nominated.

Mark didn't bother watching on television. The convention would be dominated by windy speeches about how great Knox and the Republican Party were. There was very little television coverage. Even the web sites weren't interested. Knox would choose his Vice Presidential candidate and each would make their predictable acceptance speeches. Mark went to his house at Pebble Beach and played golf. He needed diversion after all these months. Besides, there was nothing more he could do.

The manager of the Cypress Point golf club hurriedly drove his golf cart to the tee of the oceanside 15th hole as Mark prepared to make his shot. "Mr. Stevens, sir, I'm sorry to interrupt your game, but President Knox has called from Los Angeles and wants to speak to you. I thought I should come to you immediately."

"You did the right thing. I assume he left a number."

Mark took the number and asked his caddy to retrieve his phone from his golf bag.

"Hello, Stuart. I wish I didn't have to say this, but congratulations on your nomination. What can I do for you?"

"I've thought long and hard about this, Mark, so don't take what I am about to say lightly."

"Oh? What is it? You have won."

"I want you to be my Vice President."

"Stuart, if I didn't know you I would think you're joking, or maybe out of your mind."

"I'm dead serious. I need your support on the ticket."

"But I don't have to tell you, it would be impossible. We have the same old disagreement about terrorism, let alone all our other differences that the campaign has brought out. You've just sloughed off the Rome bombing. There will be more attacks to come."

"Look, Kennedy and Johnson had huge differences, but Kennedy wanted Johnson as V.P. and together they won."

"No, Stuart. You flatter me, I guess, but the answer is, 'no.'"

"But we would unite the party. Together we couldn't lose."

Mark paused. He wanted to be polite to the President of the United States, but he was seething inside. This man was nothing more than a complete politician seeking to retain power. "Stuart, my answer is, 'no.' Irrevocably, 'no!'"

Mark returned to the golf tee. His errant shot squirted to the right and threatened to go into the ocean. The nerve of that man, he thought. He only wished there was something he could do about the situation.

Then the thought suddenly came him. He could still run for President.

He would have to sleep on it. Sudden inspirations were not always the right thing to do. This would require some serious thought.

Making the race into a three-man contest? Forming a third party? Would he have a chance to win? Would it be a waste of energy and the money he knew it would take? Would he be labeled a sore loser? Would it be to the best interest of his country? Soon he would have to decide.

CHAPTER TWENTY-TWO

The next morning as Jorge drove the old Rolls the 100 odd miles from Pebble Beach to Nob Hill, Mark was in the passenger compartment thinking about yesterday's inspiration and the questions it raised. He dialed Christina. It would be evening in Italy. She would be having dinner in her villa—probably alone as was her custom, her chance to think after her usual busy day at *Il Verita*.

"Christina, dear." He didn't identify himself. "I've got this crazy idea. I may form a third party and run for President on my own." His enthusiasm was evident. "What do you think?"

"I don't think it's crazy at all. We've had many parties here ever since I can remember. Perhaps it's not the best, but it works for us."

"But, you see, I'd not have any members in Congress as your parties have. I'd only be President."

"What do you mean you'd *only* be President? You'd have tremendous power. At least as I understand your system."

"You're right. Not the least of which would be Commander-In-Chief of the armed forces."

"Haven't the United States had many Presidents who didn't have a majority in your Congress? You could still wield a great deal of power," Christina observed.

Her attitude contributed to his enthusiasm for the whole idea. "Yes, if I won the Presidency, Congress would have to pay attention to me. Democrats and Republicans alike. It would shake up the whole government. All the naysayers."

They talked for much of his trip back to San Francisco, before saying their goodbyes.

How would he go about this? There would be a million things to think about. Decisions to be made. Would he have a chance to win? He was confident that a great many Democrats would vote for him. Their candidate, John Morgan, was a nothing. A man with little chance to win. Probably many, even most, of the Republicans who voted for Mark in the primaries would vote for him. Maybe even plenty of those Republicans had misgivings, but had stuck with Knox, would switch over. As the big old car pulled into the Nob Hill garage, Mark was filled with eager enthusiasm. He wanted to get going.

The telephone call was from William Peterson, the chair of the Republican National Committee. "President Knox has a request of you."

"Oh?" Mark responded warily.

"The President would like you to address the L.A. convention. Oh, I know it's unconventional for a candidate to speak before the vote, but he thinks it would be a sign of party unity if you spoke."

"Oh. No. The President knows I cannot endorse him. I don't know if he told you, but he offered me the Vice Presidency."

"I know. You don't have to endorse him, but it would be a sign that you believe in the party principles."

"I'm sorry, but I have to decline."

"Will you at least think about it? And, maybe, call me tomorrow?"

"Okay, I'll call you as a matter of courtesy."

"Give it serious thought."

Mark telephoned Christina, Rodney and Rolf to tell them of his decision about forming a third party. Mark told Rodney of the invitation to speak at the convention. "That gives me an idea" said Rolf, "I'm coming to San Francisco tomorrow for a morning court appearance. Let's have lunch together. You may like my brainstorm."

"Good. Let's meet at the Pacific Union Club. How about 12:30?"

"See you there."

They had lunch while Rolf explained his brainstorm. Mark liked his friend's idea. He liked it very much. The use of cell phones was not allowed at the dining room of the club, but, when lunch was over, Mark stepped into a phone booth off the lobby and called William Peterson. "I've changed my mind. I will speak at the convention before the vote is taken."

"Wonderful. I'll call the President right away with the good news. He'll be very pleased."

Mark was quite certain that when his speech to the convention was over, Knox wouldn't think it was such good news."

CHAPTER TWENTY-THREE

The Republican National Convention in Los Angeles had tediously droned on for two days. The city had been chosen because downtown Los Angeles had experienced a very strong revitalization in the last 35 or more years. Once a downtown that was deserted in the evenings, it was now rivaling many of the great downtowns of the world. It was for that reason that the Republican National Committee had chosen the city for its convention. Republicans wanted to be identified with prosperity. TV coverage of the routine proceedings previously had been virtually non-existent, although the contrary was true of the Internet.

The big news announced by the party Chairman was that Mark Stevens would address the convention tonight. For a candidate to give speech before the voting was highly unconventional. Thus the speech gave rise to excitement. Television would cover the event.

Speculation was rampant. Would Stevens support the President so as to unify the party? Despite the rumor that Stevens had turned down Knox's invitation to be his

Vice President, would he announce a change of mind? Or would he simply concede the obvious, that Knox would be nominated?

There were no empty chairs tonight. As Stevens stood on the podium there was, at first, silence. Then the entire arena burst into cheering and applause. The crowd recognized that the man had honest differences with the President and had waged an exhausting campaign. Stevens had lost, but he had made his mark. The cheering lasted for all of five minutes, despite Mark's continual efforts to quiet the crowd.

"To my fellow Republicans here in the hall," he began. "And of equal, perhaps of more importance, I speak to the many independents and undecided Democrats across the nation."

Strange for him to make this last statement, many thought. This was a Republican convention.

"Throughout this campaign I have tried to set forth my honest opinion about many issues that, no doubt, many, if not most of you in this convention disagree with. Gay marriage, or at least the rights of gays to have recognition. Reformation of Medicare and Social Security, abortion and the Supreme Court, elimination of farm subsidies, government assistance to stem cell research and several others. You may very well disagree with many of my stances, but I think you understand that I am not pandering to you. I confess to you that I remain puzzled that conservatives feel free to regulate private so-called moral conduct of its citizens, but abhor government interference with economic matters.

"The important thing is that all these issues were, and remain, side issues. The important issue—the only real vital issue—is terrorism! This nation has been asleep to this new al Qaeda threat. As a cabinet member, I repeatedly warned the President. But no real attention was paid to my warnings. I presented proof that the threat was real. But the President, his administration, indeed the public remained unconvinced—even indifferent. All refused to look at the unpleasant truth. So I resigned as Secretary of the Treasury. You know, if you have been paying attention to my campaign, that for months I proclaimed I was not running for your nomination. I didn't want to be President. I was campaigning to warn the nation of what I knew to be the truth.

"Then this new al Qaeda blew up the American embassy in Rome. What happened? The leader of al Qaeda said he was sorry, it was all a mistake, it wasn't his group, it must have been another group. Did you believe him?" Most of Mark's delegates in the room let out with a very loud "No!" "But not so with President Knox. He simply didn't want to be realistic. What about the Democratic leaders? The same thing! Have I failed in my mission?" Again a loud "No!" from Mark's supporters. "I'm sorry, but despite your enthusiasm I have failed. This convention is going to nominate Stuart Knox to be President. I do not have enough votes to change that fact."

The convention was silent, except for some mild buzzing. What was he saying? We all knew all of this. Why say it? This was not a message of unification. This was not a message of support for Knox. Stevens was not going to accept the nomination for Vice President. Even his supporters wondered why did Stevens choose to speak before the convention? What was the point?

"So what am I to do?" Mark asked. "I could go back to my beloved San Francisco. I could look at the beautiful Golden Gate Bridge from my window. I could sharpen my golf game at the Monterey peninsula. I could look at the Pacific Ocean and listen to the barking of the sea lions."

There was no sound in the hall.

"But that is not the way Mark Stevens is built. I cannot sit idly by and wait for another September 11, 2001. To ladies and gentlemen of this convention, to those of you watching on television, to Mr. Assad plotting on his little island in the Pacific. I hereby announce that I am running for President of the United States of America. Yes, I am this day forming a third party. I have decided to name it the Lincoln Party. This party will be named after the only third party candidate in history to actually win the election and become the President of the United States. Yes, Lincoln and the Republican Party that nominated him was a minority party.

"I have new evidence that has made me all the more resolute. The British Government has just discovered that the money for this new threat—the money for the bombing in Rome—has been supplied from a source in London. Further that source has just fled to Tamar and still controls vast resources. I'm telling you tonight that I have no doubt that Assad and this newly discovered source are plotting new attacks on our nation as I speak to you!

"What will I do as President? I will squelch this threat. First there will be negotiation with the King of that small island, then, if that doesn't work, there will be economic sanctions, followed by other measures. And finally, if none of these efforts succeeds there will be invasion. This threat must be stopped! That is why I am running for President of the United States."

There was some applause, apparently from Mark's delegates, but most of the members of the convention sat in stunned silence as Mark left the podium.

CHAPTER TWENTY-FOUR

While Mark was addressing the convention, Derek Hardin's plane landed unexpectedly at the Tamar airport. Assad rushed to the plane to meet him. They walked briskly to Assad's tiny office.

"I had to leave Britain at once. I discovered the authorities were about to arrest me. Apparently the government knows I've been financing you and your operation. All I have with me is what I could quickly get on my jet."

Assad had never seen Derek so shaken. He actually seemed human, rather than the usually cool-headed tyrant barking orders.

"We'll get you into one of the King's seaside villas. You'll be quite comfortable there, I'm sure."

"Don't worry about my money supply. I have everything set up so that I have access to all my accounts and assets, particularly those outside of the U.K. I have always anticipated the possibility of such an event," Derek blurted.

"Good. I'm pleased to have you here, my friend."

Derek smiled, apparently relieved. Friend to Assad, he was not, but the man was essential to the organization. Assad continued: "I have been watching the Internet. Apparently we're about to see Stevens making an important speech to the Republicans in Los Angeles."

Together they watched the delayed transmission of Mark's speech to the Republican National Convention.

When the speech was over, they looked at one another. "So he's actually going to try to be President, commented Assad. "This means the battle lines have been drawn." Assad paused. "What will we do if he's actually elected?"

"Don't worry. He won't be elected. None of the candidates will ever be elected."

"What do you mean? How can we stop them?" Assad saw how quickly Hardin changed from a shaken man to his accustomed confident, assertive self.

"The reason I was opposed to the bombing in Rome was because of the plan I have formulated. I tell you now, none of the candidates, including Stevens, will be around to be elected," said Derek.

"Not be around?"

"You see, old man, I am quite certain there has never been a dead man elected to be President of the United States!"

* * *

It would be seven months of campaigning before the November election. But before the exhausting campaign, Mark decided to have a few weeks away. He wanted to see Christina, maybe meet some of the leaders in Europe and Asia. He would need to establish his credentials in foreign policy and, if he were elected, he'd want to gain foreign support to deal with the Tamar problem. Perhaps Christina would find time to join him on his journeys.

As usual, Christina met him at the airport in her vintage convertible Ferrari. As always her long blond hair trailed behind her as they sped to her villa. Mark assumed she had her hair colored, but it didn't matter.

"I'm thrilled that you decided to continue your run for the Presidency. As I told you, we in Italy are quite used to having more than two parties in the race. Your two-party system seems rather odd to most of us."

"It has served us quite well over the years, but not this time," said Mark.

"To be quite realistic, do you think you have a chance to win?" she asked. He had to strain to hear her over the wind as she sped through the traffic.

"We shall see," he told her. "We shall see."

Without Mark's asking, she drove by the boarded ruins of the American Embassy. The scene made an impact on Mark. "I'm making a vow to the American people that we shall put an end to this violence," he said sternly.

Although it was not the same as when they were young, they made love often in their limited time together. He reveled in the simple joy of being with her. Christina was the love of his life. Sharing the same bed, having breakfast together, walking the villa's grounds hand in hand was more joy than he had known in past years.

Her newspaper duties were such that she would not be able to join him on his trips to meet the world leaders.

Mark assumed that if he won the White House, she would only be able to be with him occasionally. *Il Verita* was her life's purpose. He could never ask her to give it up, even if she might consent. When they said goodbye at the airport, Mark felt rejuvenated. He was ready to do what he had to do to win the presidency.

On the way from the airport back to *Il Verita* Christina found herself wondering. What if her beloved man—this Mark Stevens, who had been in and out of her life over the years—what if he became Mark Stevens, President of the United States of America? What if he asked her to move to Washington? What if he asked her to marry him? What would her answer be? Well, she thought, those were questions she did not need to answer, at least not now.

She pulled the Ferrari into the garage and shut off the motor. She had work to do. There had been important events in the American elections, and she needed to write her weekly Saturday editorial.

* * *

The visits to the foreign capitals went off without a hitch. The media followed his every stop. Mark Stevens was not a one-issue candidate. That was the purpose of this exercise.

Mark spent a few days in London before returning to the U.S. "Rodney, I want to thank you for ferreting out our old enemy Derek. How did you ever manage it?"

"Old friends, my dear fellow. An old friend from Oxford is in the government, a rather high post in Whitehall. That is what old friends, especially Oxford friends, are for, you know."

Then, on to New York. Mark spent time with his political consultants, mapping out his campaign stops and arranging for media coverage. Not that media coverage needed much arranging. The press was following his every step. He was perceived as a viable third party candidate. The Lincoln Party. This was news. Real news.

As he had expected, the next months before the election were to be a severe grind. But he had survived the primary campaigning for the nomination, so he could handle this. In fact the crowds rejuvenated him as he went from state to state. Yes, he understood that the enthusiasm was coming from people who supported him, but he needed their lively juice. His campaign flooded television and the Internet with his ads.

* * *

The campaign was coming to a close. There would be but one debate. In past years the several debates had tended to be repetitive, but more importantly, the Secret Service felt it safer for there to be just the one. It would be nine days before the November Election Day. It would be a vital cap to the months of campaigning. Commentators agreed that the performances could make the difference in the outcome. True, they observed, polls tended to show that Stevens and his Lincoln Party were tending to split the Republican vote and might result in the election of the Democrat, John Morgan. Historians on talk shows reminded their listeners, that Woodrow Wilson had been elected in the 1900s because, even though former President Theodore Roosevelt and his Bull Moose Party had more votes than the Republican incumbent, President Taft, he had split the Republican vote giving the election to Wilson. On the other hand pundits pointed out the polls showed that Stevens was appealing to thousands of independents and also Democrats who felt that the terrorist threat was very real and that Stevens could best deal with it. Perhaps, they opined, Stevens could pull it off.

Weeks earlier, on Tamar Derek Hardin and Assad were perfecting their conspiracy. The reason the bombing in Rome was successful, Assad pointed out, was that the tiny, yet powerful bombs were so technologically sophisticated that they had been implanted in strategic spots in the embassy and had remained undetected. They had been implanted months before the fateful day that they had been detonated by remote devices from some distance.

But the issue here was that there was no way it could be learned where the only Presidential debate would be held. The Secret Service insisted that the location of the debate be kept secret. In fact the protectors of the three candidates would not know it until the day before the event. Even then agents would be assigned to the other possible debate sites, so as to deceive possible plotters.

But the conspirators had had a plan to outwit the Secret Service. The devices would be implanted as early as May to make it easier to avoid detection. But what location would they zero in on? If they guessed wrong the plot would fail. Their solution: choose several possible locations and be prepared to detonate them all, if it were necessary. Assad's henchmen in America choose likely locations in selected cities. There had been a history of the moderator, for many of the debates, to be a commentator from Public Television. They reasoned that the Secret Service would likely decide to bar attendance by the public to minimize the risk. Finally the terrorists chose three Public Television Studios: Boston, Washington and New York as targets.

It was now November and the explosive devices had been in place for some time.

CHAPTER TWENTY-FIVE

The three Presidential candidates each diligently prepared for the debate in their respective headquarters. Mark in New York, Knox in Washington and Morgan in Chicago. It was unknown to each, where they would fly for the debate tonight. Each had practiced the entire day. Morgan had been preparing for three days now because he was not an effective debater.

The polls showed that Morgan was trailing Mark, but Knox had the lead, at least according to the polls taken last week. Each had independently decided to wear conservative dark suits with bold striped ties, the political uniform of the day. The campaigns had expressed disappointment that the number of debates had been reduced to one, but that they had deferred to the Secret Service. Mark was happy with the decision. He didn't know when the next attack would occur, but what better time for al Qaeda to mount an attack than just before the election?

The word from the Secret Service came late. It would be the studio of Boston Public Television. Assad's men had guessed correctly—one of the major PBS stations.

All three debaters took their positions on stage. The Secret Service had been on alert at several locations throughout the nation, but, it had been a diversionary tactic. Boston had been secretly selected a month ago.

As television took to the air, the moderator laid out the ground rules of the debate. Ten minutes for each opening statement, followed by short questioning from the other candidates, etc.

"The entire process will end at 90 minutes. Gentlemen, please keep your statements and answers to the point. Before we conclude you will each be given 15 minutes to summarize your positions on the issues. Gentlemen, a few minutes ago each of your representatives drew a number for you. Mr. Stevens, you are to commence followed by President Knox and then Mr. Morgan. Mr. Stevens you have ten minutes. Please begin."

"Ladies and Gentlemen, the main reason I am running for President is that I am convinced that the threat of terrorism is more real than it has ever been. I believe that I am better equipped than my opponents to deal with this threat. I have been warning of it for well over a year now. It is only lately that my opponent, President Knox, has taken me at all seriously—and then only half-heartedly." Mark used the balance of his time to briefly outline his positions on various other issues. But he emphasized that terrorism was the main issue.

Knox was the first to begin the questioning of Mark. "As you know, Mr. former Secretary, with the exception of the rogue attack in Rome, there has been no terrorist activity for many years—"

Then it happened. The explosive devices in the Boston television studio were detonated with an ear-piercing explosion.

Simultaneously the ceiling collapsed on the participants. The stage buckled beneath the candidates and moderator. First upward, and then downward. Dust flew everywhere. The TV cameras were tossed aside. The moderator collapsed on the heaving floor. The three candidates all but disappeared in the debris and dust. The dreaded event had destroyed the debate and apparently had ended the entire election process.

Those of the Secret Service who were still alive rushed toward the stage through the wreckage. All were choking with dust, climbing around and over debris. Were the candidates alive or were they dead? At the very least, certainly, all three were badly wounded. The scene was pandemonium and filled with fear!

Across the nation televisions and Internet pictures went blank. "What had happened?" was the question being asked by millions.

There was an interminable delay, before the TV picture came back on. A shaken voice took the air. "Ladies and Gentlemen this is Michael Grossman in New York. We do not know what has happened, but obviously it is very serious." Grossman paused, trying to collect himself. An off-camera hand gave the emotional TV announcer a piece of paper.

"Ladies and Gentlemen, this just in. Reports are in from several cities. Explosions have occurred in possible, but unused, debate settings in various Public Television studios across the nation. We have a report from Washington. Another from New York. There may be others. I'm sorry, but I cannot go on. A major catastrophe has occurred." The disturbed announcer dabbed at his eyes with his hand, then with a tissue handed to him.

Another figure appeared on the screen. He wore the clothing of a technician. "We don't know what has happened. We are frantically searching for a possible bomb here in Chicago." The man sat before the camera, speechless and frightened. "Please, some other station in our network, take the air. Please!" Suddenly the TV screens across the nation again went blank, leaving their viewers still in shock.

A wounded Secret Service agent shouted into his cell phone to the crew of the standby ambulances waiting outside the Boston studio. "Get in here immediately. Get as many paramedics and ambulances as possible. Call the morgue! Right now! Do you hear me? For God's sake!" He was speaking sternly and clearly, while clearly shaken.

The paramedics made their way through the settling dust and rubble to what had been the stage. They had to ignore the bodies of the dead and cries of the wounded in order to get to the three candidates, or at least what was left of them. First was President Knox. He appeared to be barely alive, mumbling something weakly. "I'm sorry. I'm sorry," he seemed to be whispering.

John Morgan was clearly dead. A beam or something equally as heavy had crushed his head. There was no sound, no pulse. Although he was dead, they would take him to the hospital.

What about Mark Stevens? The crew working on him removed piece after piece of broken rubble. His white hair was covered with blood. He did not respond to the paramedics, but he had a pulse. Yes, he was alive!

All three were put on gurneys and rushed from the rubble. Additional paramedics turned to the other wounded, dying and dead. The Boston ambulances were worked to their full capacity. The search through the shambles would continue. Finally television and Internet screens throughout the nation came to life. Few of them were public television outlets in major cities—most had been totally decimated as in Boston.

Along with many of the White House staff, President Knox's Chief of Staff, Harry Manning, had been watching the debate in the West Wing.

"Damned TV" Manning shouted.

"It seems all right now," his secretary uttered.

"What has happened?" was the question all were asking

"Shh," someone blurted as a harried announcer began.

"Ladies and Gentlemen, we have lost contact with the debate in Boston. We don't know the cause. Wait! We have a live camera outside the studio standing by the President's limousine. We switch there. I'm sorry sir, but I don't know your name. What has happened?"

"I'm not with the television people. Your man is inside. I'm Jeffrey Baines." The man was adjusting the unfamiliar headset. "I'm with the Secret Service. I'm the President's driver."

"What do you see, Mr. Baines?"

"The studio is completely demolished. It was a series of bombs." The man was nearly breathless. "Ambulances arrived some minutes ago and the paramedics rushed inside. Wait! Here are some paramedics coming out now! My God they have three men on gurneys!"

"Who are they?"

"I'm sorry, I can't talk anymore."

The camera pointed aimlessly. Switching about with no apparent goal. A voice appeared. "This is Dick Myer. I'm the cameraman. We have no announcer! Just a minute. I'll try to tell you what I see. Sir! Sir! Can you tell me what happened? Who do you have on that gurney? My God, I can see myself. It's President Knox! Tell me sir, is the President alive?"

"Yes. I think so, but just barely. We're taking him to the hospital now. Please get out of the way." Apparently it was a medic speaking.

"The President had blood all over his face," the cameraman continued. "He was very pale. I thought he was dead when I first saw him. I don't know. He may be dead. My God, what a terrible catastrophe! I don't know if I can continue." There was a long silence.

"Try another channel," shouted Manning. Now there was a picture of the ambulances and the medics wheeling two more bodies to waiting ambulances.

"I don't know who is on the gurneys. But, I repeat, President Knox has been put in an ambulance. It has sped off along with two Secret Service vehicles. No doubt, they are taking the President to the closest hospital. I assume it's Massachusetts General. I know the Secret Service has already selected a hospital wherever the President is traveling. I'm only guessing it's Mass General. Let me see if these other two are Mark Stevens and the Democratic candidate, John Morgan. There are several more ambulances waiting and I hear the sirens of even more coming, off in the distance. My God, what a catastrophe. What a catastrophe!"

"This is John Billings in New York," said a familiar anchor. Our news reports from all over the nation are telling us of explosions in various Public Television studios in their cities. My God, it appears that Secretary Stevens was correct in his assertions that al Qaeda attacks were likely to happen at any time. According to our reports the nation is in chaos. . . . One moment please. We now switch you to the White House."

"Ladies and Gentlemen, stand by for the Vice President of the United States."

The screen was blank for several seconds, very long seconds.

"This is Roberto Mendez, your Vice President," said the serious looking and all but unknown Vice President of the United States. "As you know, there has been a disaster in Boston. I have been in communication with the Secret Service in Massachusetts General Hospital. They have the latest medical report on the condition of President Knox. I must report to you that his condition is very grave. I have consulted with Attorney General Phillips, who is of the opinion that I should be ready to initiate the procedures set forth in the Twenty-Fifth Amendment to the Constitution to assume the duties of the President as therein set forth." It was obvious that the shaken Mendez was reading from a teleprompter. "My fellow Americans, never in our long history have we faced a constitutional crisis of this import. As you know, the election is next week. The import of this dastardly deed on that election is unknown at this time." The Vice President mopped his brow with a handkerchief handed to him. "I shall call a cabinet meeting in a few hours. By then we will know more about the condition of the President and, of course, the other two candidates. This will also give the Attorney General and his advisors more opportunity to study the ramifications of this tragedy. I will see to it that all of you are kept apprised of the condition of our President. In the meantime, I suggest that each of you, no matter what religion, pray for our nation."

"Ladies and Gentlemen," said the New York television anchor. "You have heard the statement of Vice President Mendez. I have just been handed a bulletin from Massachusetts General Hospital. It reports that the Democratic candidate John Morgan was pronounced 'dead on arrival.' His fatal wounds were massive. Apparently he was killed instantly, either from the blast itself or from collapsing debris." The announcer was distracted by something off-camera. "We have no report about the condition of Secretary Stevens, except that he, apparently, is alive."

At the White House, Harry Manning half stumbled to the television and changed the channel. Though Chief of Staff to Knox, he had not been consulted by the President before Philips had been chosen as his running mate four years ago solely to balance the Republican ticket. He was angered because the President had ignored him. Manning was closer to Knox than any other person. Philips was a nobody Governor from Texas who had been selected merely to balance the ticket. Harry Manning intensely disliked the man.

Next, the television showed a discussion by four political commentators who were already analyzing the meaning of the disaster. Manning was annoyed that such a discussion was taking place, but he was a political animal and couldn't help but listen.

"It's obvious that Stevens knew what he was talking about," said the first to speak.

"My guess is that the conspirators did not know where the debate was to be held, so they planted devices in several locations where the debate might be held."

"Amazing. I would have thought that the Secret Service would have conducted a sweep, at least of the Boston studio."

"Well, even the Secret Service didn't know where the debate was to be held."

"Yes, but I'm sure they swept as soon as they found out."

"No doubt the bombs were hidden months ago, in anticipation."

"Yes, undetectable, as in the Rome Embassy."

"But what happens next? The election is to be held next week."

"Even if President Knox and Secretary Stevens survive, surely Stevens has the advantage now."

"But the sympathy vote is going to be there."

"Sympathy? You'd think more for the President than Stevens. But after all Stevens, we now know, was right about the threat."

Manning turned off the television in disgust—or was it that he feared for is own future?

CHAPTER TWENTY-SIX

It was early in the morning of the second day since the disaster. The nation remained in a state of shock and confusion. What would happen next? What would the future hold for America? On television, the Internet, wherever people gathered, nothing else was talked about. The highways and streets were very lightly traveled. Stock markets were closed, businesses absenteeism was high and most could have closed for all anyone cared.

Ironically, Mark and the President were in adjacent rooms in the Intensive Care Unit at Massachusetts General. Additional Secret Service had been flown in. Everyone was checked and watched, including the medical personnel.

The medical staff had worked competently and feverishly over the two patients. "I'm afraid, I don't have much hope for the President's survival," said the Chief Surgeon in charge. The poor man's body was hopelessly crushed. We've done all we can do."

"I have to agree," said his assistant. "There's no point in further mangling his body. His breathing is getting much worse."

"Doctor, the President's heart rate is dangerously low," warned the nurse.

"It's just a matter of time. A very short time," the Chief Surgeon responded.

His analysis was correct. It was a very short time, indeed, when the monitor showed no pulse. The heart had stopped. The President of the United States was dead.

The authorities had to be notified. The body would be flown to Washington on Air Force One, where an autopsy would be performed and arrangements made for the pageantry of a Presidential funeral. It had been a long time since a President had died in office—1963—John Fitzgerald Kennedy.

The President's body had been removed. In the next room Mark stirred. For the entire time Mark had been unconscious from the blow to his head. Slowly he opened his eyes. Fuzzy figures seemed to surround him. His eyes began to focus. "Christina?" he mumbled.

"Yes Mark, I'm here," she answered.

Mark turned his bandaged head slightly. "Rodney?" He turned slightly more. "Rolf?"

"Yes, we're all here," said Christina.

"Am I alive?"

Christina took his hand and gently kissed it.

"What happened? Am I in a hospital?"

"The entire story will have to wait until later, my old friend," said Rolf. "The doctor doesn't want you to talk. You nearly died."

"No, I want to hear what happened."

"But the doctor said—" said Rodney"

"To hell with that! What happened? Tell me!"

Rolf told him about the destruction. "You've been unconscious for two days. You're lucky to be alive."

Mark's head had cleared. "What about Morgan, what about Knox?

"Bad news I'm afraid," said Rolf. "Morgan was killed instantly."

"And Knox? Is he okay? Is the President alive or what?"

"I'm afraid President Knox didn't make it. The doctors did everything they could. This is a wonderful hospital with a wonderful staff. But the President passed away less than an hour ago."

"My God!" Mark nearly shouted as he tried to get up.

"No. No. You must stay in bed," ordered Christina.

"But what are we going to do? The nation! The election! My Lord!" Mark's voice was surprisingly strong.

"I don't know what they're going to do about the election," said Rolf. "Nothing like this has ever happened. But, for now, you've got to be quiet. Your body has to have time to recover. We are all lucky you survived."

"The President. Is he still here? His body?"

"No. They've taken him to Logan—to Air Force One—to fly him back to Washington."

"What a mess!" said Mark. "What a mess!"

Thousands of miles away Derek and Assad had been gleefully watching the news on the Internet in Derek's villa.

"We've made September 11th look like child's play," said Assad.

"Yes, Morgan, and now the President are dead," said Derek. "But what about Stevens. Did we get the bloody bastard?"

"I'm sure we did. Nobody could have survived that blast."

"But we have no reports."

"Don't worry, we got him, I'm sure," said Assad.

"I hope you're right."

"We've killed hundreds, maybe thousands. That will wake up that evil giant. The whole damn United States is in turmoil."

"Yes, but I won't be satisfied until we know we got Stevens. That's what I've been planning for months now. I hate the man. I hate the whole country." Hardin's face was red.

Mark was still in the hospital. Christina, Rolf and Rodney remained constantly pacing the corridors and then taking turns at the bedside. It was clear now, that Mark would survive. It was also clear that the doctors would insist that he remain in the hospital.

The election would take place next Tuesday, unless Congress delayed the date. And it was doubtful that it could even meet before Tuesday, let alone agree to what should be done.

The Chief Justice in a hasty private ceremony in the Vice President's mansion swore in Vice President Mendez to be President. No television was allowed. Mendez wanted to show respect for the dead President. He intended to follow the Presidential caisson to Arlington Cemetery. What a weird set of circumstances. The President would be buried in a very few days after his successor was elected. Yet in fact Mendez was his successor, but only until January.

The Chairman of the Republican National Committee called a meeting in Washington. Its members flew in from all over the country. The party rules provided that, in the unlikely event of the death of the Republican candidate, the Committee would choose his successor to be the Republican candidate.

"What more logical candidate than Roberto Mendez?" said the Chairman. After all he is the Vice President."

"No. Not the Vice President. He is the President of the United States. We have no better candidate."

Harry Manning was a member of the Committee. Many months ago Manning had been selected as the representative of President Knox. Manning angrily spoke up: "Logical candidate my foot! Mendez was nothing more than a figurehead. Knox chose him merely for political reasons. He never participated in any White House decisions. He was to make speeches and go to funerals. That's it."

"Well, Harry, who do you suggest? My God, man, the election takes place next Tuesday. Stuart's name will still be on the ballot."

"I think it's obvious who Harry wants to suggest," said another committee member. "I know of no other person who has more inside information and who knows the policies of Stuart more than Chief of Staff Harry Manning. We all know Mendez is a nothing."

"I stand ready to serve in this crisis," volunteered Manning.

The debate went on for nearly two hours, when finally a motion was made and the question called.

"I think we would be foolish to select anyone other than Mendez. After all he is the sitting President. He has the same political qualifications that Stuart saw in him. Sorry, Harry. But Roberto gives us the best chance to win Tuesday, despite all this chaos."

A second was made to the motion. The vote for Mendez was unanimous, except for Harry Manning who stormed out of the meeting. He knew that no matter what happened Tuesday, he would soon be out of a job with not an ounce of power left to his name.

The next day a similar meeting was held in the Democratic National Committee. Some years ago the Committee had decided to adopt the same procedure as the Republicans for choosing a candidate in the event of death of a candidate. The meeting was held with a lack of enthusiasm for another candidate. Before the disaster in Boston, it had been felt by most that the only chance the Democrats had to win was that Stevens would split the Republican vote, resulting in a Democratic victory. Now the whole situation was up for grabs. Most Committee members felt that there was no strong Democratic candidate. Ultimately the members decided to follow the path set by the Republicans and decided upon their Vice Presidential candidate, Milton Robards. Robards was a Senator from the State of Washington and was as good as any as a substitute candidate. At least Robards had become known as he campaigned throughout the large states.

It was Tuesday—Election Day. The confused, saddened, voters trooped to the polls—those who had not mailed in absentee ballots. Turnout was low. It was the dreariest, oddest Presidential Election in the nation's long history.

CHAPTER TWENTY-
SEVEN

In Massachusetts General Hospital Mark was well enough to watch the election returns trickle in. His head wound still bandaged, they had moved him into a suite where he sat in an easy chair. Christina, Rolf and Rodney were with him, watching the TV.

Christina had been in constant contact with her newspaper. She had submitted several stories about the disaster and ensuing events.

The first election reports, as usual, came from New Hampshire. Apparently Mark had won that state. Then the votes began pouring in after the polls had closed in the Eastern Time Zone. Results were mixed and confusing. Later the Central Time Zone votes became available. Illinois was late in supplying its final count, but so far in Illinois, the Republican, Mendez had more votes than either Mark or Robards, the Democrat. It was expected that the Chicago vote would favor the Democrat. So far a large percentage of the votes were for the two candidates who were now dead. There had been no time to place the substitute names on the ballots. Mark was running strongly, but falling well short of 50%.

The television reporting turned to a panel of experts. "It is obvious that many voters were confused, but the bombings clearly have convinced a large number of voters to vote for Stevens. After all he was right about the terrorists," noted the anchor.

"We need to make clear that legally the voters are not voting for the candidates, dead or alive. Voters have actually voted for Electors to the Electoral College," explained another member of the panel. "Under the Constitution it is the majority of the Electors who will ultimately select the President. Not actually the voters directly. Therefore, the newly selected Republican and Democratic substitute candidates will presumably get the Electors originally pledged to President Knox and John Morgan, the Democrat," said another panelist.

"But it remains in doubt—at least at this point— whether any candidate will receive a majority of the Electors."

"Yes, a majority is required by the Constitution—to be President."

"But what happens if no one receives a majority? Is there a run-off election?"

"No run-off. If no one gets a majority, the winner is elected by the House of Representatives."

"I had forgotten that."

"Yes, I believe it's the 12th Amendment. If I remember my history it happened once before under the 12th Amendment."

"Who? Abraham Lincoln?" the conversation continued.

"No, it was John Quincy Adams. It was the election of 1824. Oh, it had happened in the 1800 election, but that was before the 12th Amendment changed the system." This panel member was a Presidential historian from the University of Michigan—a man who had made many TV appearances on Public Television over the years, but now, with the destruction of three important PBS stations, was making this appearance on a commercial channel.

"It still seems very confusing to me. I thank you for the clarification. I guess I should go back to my Political Science college textbook," the anchor half-joked.

Mark and his friends sat glued to the television, occasionally changing channels.

It was past midnight in Boston. The TV reported that the election results were all but completed, with 98% of the vote counted. "The Electoral count is as follows," said the TV anchor. "Of the 538 at stake, no one, no party, has a majority. Stevens has 221. Mendez, the Republican has 189. Robards, the Democrat has 121, although the counts in Oregon, Washington and Florida are very close. We may not know the results in those states until tomorrow."

Another commentator spoke: "Yes, but even when the final count in those states is known, it will not change the result. No one will have a majority of the Electors."

"And this means—?"

"Yes, it means that when the final votes of the Electoral College are counted by the Congress, there will be no winner. The matter will then go to the House for a decision."

"Folks, in anticipation of this, our staff has prepared a copy of the relevant part of the Constitution," said the anchor. "We will now show it on the screen and I shall read it aloud as our listeners read it for themselves."

> *"Amendment XII to the Constitution (in part):*
>
> *"The President of the Senate shall, in the presence of the Senate and House of Representatives, open all the certificates of the Electors and the votes shall be counted . . . and if no person have such a majority . . . the House of Representatives shall choose immediately, by ballot, the President. But in choosing the President, the votes shall be taken by states, the representation from each state having one vote . . . a majority of all states shall be necessary to a choice."*

"Sounds awfully complicated to me," said a panel member. "Could you tell me what it means in layman's terms?"

"Well, in a nutshell, after being sworn next January, the new Senate and House meet and watch the Electoral College ballots tabulated. If no one gets a majority the House immediately, in closed door session, selects the new President."

"And whoever gets the most votes of the three wins."

"No, that is the point of the 12th Amendment. Each state House delegation meets separately and chooses how that state is going to vote. Each separate state's vote is decided by majority votes. You see, it's not a majority of the House, it's the majority of the states."

"So there are only, in effect, 50 votes?"

"Right—one vote for each state. The winner must get the vote of 26 states."

"Complicated, for sure."

"I guess you could say that, but that's what the Constitution says."

"But with three candidates, what if no one gets 26 votes?"

The professor chuckled, "Then the process is repeated until someone gets the 26 votes."

"That could take forever."

"Sure could. It took several ballots before John Quincy Adams was chosen."

"Well, thank you Professor. Do you have any opinion as to whom will be selected?"

"Only a guess. But I point out to you that apparently the Republicans have a majority in the House. A slim one over the Democrats, but a majority nevertheless. I remind you that Stevens' Lincoln party had no candidates for Congress, so his chances might be pretty slim."

"Yes, but he could be a compromise choice."

"And remember, just because the Republicans will have a majority in the new House, doesn't mean they'll have a majority of the votes in the necessary 26 states."

"Yes. And I assume some, maybe many, Republicans will vote for Stevens. After all, he is a Republican.

"And we're not going to know who will be President until the new Congress is sworn in on January 3rd.

"What a mess!"

"What a mess, indeed," agreed Mark. "Turn the damn TV off!" he asked.

CHAPTER TWENTY-EIGHT

"There has not been a funeral of a sitting President since John F. Kennedy was assassinated in 1963," said the commentator. The TV picture showed the caisson, carrying President Stuart Knox's flag draped casket, leaving the Capitol toward Arlington Cemetery. The traditional riderless horse accompanied the caisson as it slowly rolled along the Mall, passing the Washington Monument, the war memorials and ultimately the Lincoln Memorial.

"The nation is in a total state of confusion. We all wonder from where the next attack will come. We understand that Secretary Stevens is watching from his hospital suite in Boston. What can be going through his mind as we watch the somber ceremony? Stevens is the one who warned of an attack. He has issued the following gracious statement: 'President Knox had the respect of all Americans and his tragic death is a blow to everyone. I am confident that our nation will regain its balance after the recent events.'"

The television picture continued, showing a heavily guarded limousine following the caisson. "We are told that former Vice President, now President Mendez, and Mrs. Knox are sitting together behind those darkened windows. What a shock the President's murder has, no doubt, been to each of them, as it has been to the nation."

"We have a report that the Knox family considered burying the President's body in his hometown, but chose Arlington only yesterday. No decision has been made as to the location of the President's library."

In her town home in Georgetown a woman in her late 30s watched the proceedings on her television. She had no close family and was alone as she watched with sadness and tears. She was to have been visited by the President upon his return from Boston. Knox had promised her that he would divorce his wife and marry her as soon as he was no longer President. She was skeptical of her lover's vow, but she loved the man and would take whatever part of him she could get. Now, she had given no thought to her future, but, along with the nation, her life had been turned upside down.

"The crowds along the funeral route are surprisingly light," continued the commentator. "Perhaps most of the stunned nation is quietly watching on television, trying to recover from the events of the last few days."

The television channels and the Internet followed the somber proceedings to Arlington and finally concluded coverage. "There will be a two hour program tonight during which a distinguished panel will discuss the ramifications of the disaster and the process that will occur when the new Congress is sworn in," said the commentator that Mark and his friends were watching.

"What next?" asked Christina.

"We just have to wait until the new Congress is sworn in January sixth to see whether the House chooses Mark to be President," Rolf answered.

"What a weird system," commented Rodney. "In the U.K. Parliament would simply choose a new P.M."

"Well, I'm not going to just sit on my ass waiting for January," said Mark standing up with difficulty from his chair.

"But what can you do?" wondered Christina.

"I'm not sure exactly, but it's clear from the election results that the new House will still be pretty well equally divided. Most of the members will be the same crowd that is already in the House."

"And I assume you intend to lobby them," said Rolf.

"Yes, and their constituents, too. I want to get public opinion on my side."

"How will you do that?" Christina asked, while assisting the tired Mark back into his chair.

Mark was short of breath as he plopped down. "The same way I campaigned on that Tuesday in February. You know the big primary day. Television. Internet. Appearances on blogs and TV shows. Everywhere I can be heard."

"Not until you're well. You have plenty of time until January, over a month," insisted Christina.

"You sound like my mother," Mark laughed.

"Maybe you need a little mothering," retorted Christina

"She's right, you know," said Rolf. "You damn near got killed less than two weeks ago. Take it easy, pal."

"But those other two guys aren't qualified to be President. I'd rather have had Knox alive than either of those two yokels."

"There will be time enough," chimed in Rodney. "There will be time."

Mark and Christina watched television that night. Rodney and Rolf had decided to return to their homes, at least for a while. Mark was out of danger now.

A television panel of four discussed the consequences of the momentous events of the last several days.

"It's clear under the Constitution we will have to wait until January sixth to know who will be our President."

"Yes, and perhaps even later. The decision may not be reached on the first ballot."

"Yes, I've been reading some history. I think that in the Jefferson-Aaron tie in the 1800 election, there were many ballots before one representative finally broke the deadlock and put Jefferson in."

"But that was before the 12th Amendment."

"But the principle is the same. However I do agree a tie is very unlikely under the 12th Amendment."

"Yes, for there to be a tie it would have to be 25 states versus 25 states."

"We're getting a little esoteric here. It would be a miracle for there to be a tie. What is required is to win 26 states or more and that would be the end of the process."

Christina interrupted the TV, "What a system! I must say I prefer our Italian system."

"I still plan to win," said Mark.

"But how?" she asked.

"Well, you see the Lincoln party, which is me, has no members in the House of Representatives. The Republicans have a slight majority and, obviously, the rest are Democrats."

"But that doesn't do you any good does it?"

"Look, I'm sure most, perhaps all, Democrats will realize their man, Robards, doesn't have a chance and they'll back me rather than giving Mendez, the Republican, the Presidency. Especially because of my various stances on a number of Democratic issues."

"So what does that mean for you? I don't understand."

"What it means, my dear, is that I've got to get enough Republican votes for me to tip the balance."

"But how can you do that?"

"Look, I've shown that I, you and I, were right about the terrorist issue. Who has the best chance of stopping further attacks? Some guy that Knox chose to be his V.P. for political reasons, or a guy named Mark Stevens who . . . well who predicted disaster."

"I see, at least I guess I do."

They were paying no attention to the television discussion.

"As soon as I get out of this damn hospital, I've got to identify the Republican members of the new House with whom I have a chance, and persuade them to vote for me."

They turned their attention back to the panelists on TV. "You see the voting in the House on January sixth will be with the doors closed. That is the law. There will be no outside campaigning. Only amongst the members themselves."

Mark clicked off the TV. "Yes," he retorted to the television. "But that won't stop me from campaigning before the voting. And that is what I intend to do."

Christina laughed. "And this from the man who didn't really want to be President."

Mark laughed along with her and pulled her to his lap.

"I'll bet you've never had sex with a man who just had a building fall on his head." In all this time since he first saw her, he had never had quite the same feelings for Christina as he had this moment.

"No, but I'm willing to try," she laughed.

CHAPTER TWENTY-NINE

For the next 30 days Mark met with many members of the House. Many had stayed in their Washington offices before breaking for the holidays. Others had returned to their districts, often making local speeches and meeting with their constituents.

Since the procedure under the 12th Amendment gave each state an equal vote, no matter their population, Mark decided to particularly concentrate on the Representatives of the thinly populated states. Wyoming with only one member of the House had a vote for President equal to California with nearly 100 members. So Mark's first order of business was to interview the Representatives of such states as Wyoming, Idaho, Delaware, New Hampshire, the Dakotas and other states with smaller House delegations. He calculated that if he could win the delegations of states such as these, he'd be well on his way toward the required 26 states and victory.

Mark's message to Democratic House members was pretty much the same. "Look, the Electoral vote is Democrats 121, Republicans 189, and my Lincoln party 221. I've split the Republican vote, so without me they can't win. The same is true of your party. Without me, they can't win. So whom would you rather have as President, Mendez, the Republican, or me? You know that I'm much closer to many of your views than Mendez. With him you'll have more of Knox."

"You've turned into quite the politician for a man who wasn't even running to win," was often the response.

"I admit it," Mark would often respond, sometimes chuckling. "But the situation has changed. Mendez is an old fashioned ultra conservative. I think I'm the better candidate to go after these terrorists and to lead the nation. Look at the popular vote I got for being a third party candidate. I was the one who warned the country about the terrorist threat. And, unfortunately, I was correct."

Mark's message to the Republican House members had a different slant. "You know Mendez can't make it without my help. He's not apt to win any Democratic states."

"Maybe so, but you can't make it without some Republican states," was the obvious response.

"I wouldn't be so sure. The Dems know they can't win with Robards. I think most of them will vote for me, before they see Mendez in the White House." Mark would repeat his point about his large popular vote and his record on the terrorist issue.

"What do you intend to do about the terrorists?"

"I'm going to take a very short time. Thirty days at the most, to try other things before force. If these other things don't work, then I'm going to bomb the hell out of Tamar and go after this terrorist group, wherever they might be."

"What 'other things' would you try before bombing Tamar?"

"We'd embargo their oil shipments, close down their financial system and, most effectively, threaten bombing and invasion. I would demand that either the U.N. or the U.S. be permitted on the island to make sure the terrorists are neutralized.

"Look, the King of Tamar and his relatives simply want to live their fat, luxurious life, collect their fancy cars, buy houses and hotels in London and Beverly Hills. With our help the King will be only too happy to throw out Assad and his so-called army.

"And if that doesn't happen? I will make good on my threats of force. I will have no hesitancy. None at all."

Despite the crisis, all of Washington shut down for the holidays. Congressmen and women were not available in their districts. The only remaining weapons at Mark's disposal during the holidays were advertising and interviews with opinion makers. Mark took full advantage of what he had. Money was no object. He blanketed the nation with electronic campaigning to get the public on his side. He urged them to write the members of Congress. By year's end there was nothing more to do, but wait for the fateful January sixth.

It was one P.M. January sixth. Mark was in the House gallery as the proceedings commenced. Rolf had flown from California to join his friend for this momentous occasion. The television crews and press were covering the events. The entire Senate was also present. The House chamber was hushed. There being no Vice President, the House Speaker presided over the counting of the Electoral College ballots that had been sent to Washington from the various states. Normally the counting would be routine with little attention being paid. Today, even though the results of this proceeding were known, what was going to happen before the evening was over was certainly not routine.

In a hushed voice a TV commentator described the proceedings to the nation. "Two Pages each carrying a wooden box of Electoral ballots are walking down the aisle. They present the boxes to the Speaker. The Speaker is opening the boxes. He and his aides are counting the ballots. Let's listen to the Speaker."

The Speaker, Donald Boyer, a Republican from Ohio, was a balding, rather rotund man. He had moved up from the Minority Leader to Speaker four years ago. "Members of Congress the results are as follows: Mr. Robards of the Democratic Party 121 votes, President Mendez of the Republican Party 189 votes and Secretary Stevens of the Lincoln Party 221 votes. Members of Congress, I hereby declare that no candidate for President has a majority of votes of the duly elected Electors. Therefore, under the 12th Amendment to the Constitution of the United States, the newly sworn members of the House of Representatives shall choose the President. Under the Amendment the voting will be by states, that is each state shall have one vote. There being 50 states it is required that the winning candidate receive the vote of 26 states. If no candidate receives said majority, additional ballots shall be taken until a candidate receives the required majority." The Speaker turned away from his prepared remarks. "The House chamber, including the gallery, shall be cleared of all persons except members of the House who shall proceed to separate themselves by the 50 states. Debate shall occur within each state delegation, followed by general debate. When all debate is concluded, a ballot shall be taken. And, as I have said, if no candidate receives a majority of 26 states, additional ballots shall be taken until we have a President."

The TV commentator continued. "All of the Senate, the pages, everyone, including ourselves, are now leaving the chamber. We shall have nothing further to report until we have a President. All I can say, as I now walk from the gallery, is that this is an amazing historical development. I return you to our studios."

It was eight P.M. The several House doors sprung open and the members began filing out. Reporters and TV commentators swarmed around them.

Mark and Rolf watched from the Georgetown townhouse as Representative Charles Rhodes of Georgia appeared on the TV camera. Rhodes was a younger, rather tall, slim man. He looked tired. "Representative Rhodes," began the interviewer, "Tell us if the House has selected a President."

"The answer is 'no', not yet. We are taking a short dinner break."

"Have you taken a ballot?"

"Yes, we have. But under the rules I cannot give you any details."

"Is the House close to electing a President?"

"I can't answer that."

"Has there been more than one ballot?"

"Sorry, but we reconvene in one hour. I cannot comment further."

"Has there been a debate?"

Rhodes laughed. "This is the House of Representatives facing a most important decision. What do you think? We're going back into session until we have a President."

Rhodes scurried away from the camera, "Thank you Representative Rhodes. Ladies and Gentlemen, there you have it. Apparently it's going to be a long night. Perhaps it will be early morning, or even tomorrow, before we have a decision."

It was two-thirty, the morning of January seventh. The House had been in session since its dinner break. The chamber's doors were suddenly opened. Has a decision been reached? The gallery was quickly filled with excited people, most from the media. Perhaps 25 Senators took seats in the front of the House chamber.

It took nearly five minutes of the Speaker pounding his gavel and calling for order, before there was quiet in the chamber. The Speaker began: "The House has reached a decision. I hereby report to the nation that our President-elect is Secretary Mark Stevens of California. Congratulations, sir. You will be sworn in at noon January 20th. A committee of members has been formed to personally notify President-elect Stevens of the results of this decision. This session is adjourned." The Speaker pounded his gavel. At first there was complete silence amongst the spectators and then there was the buzzing of conversation.

The media rushed for the main floor to interview the House members as they exited the chamber.

"Representative Robertson, could we have a word?" asked the TV reporter. Robertson was a younger looking man whose district was in the San Francisco Bay area. He was a Democrat. Mark and Rolf moved to the edges of their chairs. Their curiosity was at a height.

"Yes, the House has lifted its ban on talking about the session."

"How many ballots did it take to get the decision?"

"Well, there were five in all. The last ballot was unanimous for Stevens."

"But what about the first four?"

"To be honest with you, I wondered if we would ever reach a decision. No one was even close to the 26, but Robards, being a Democrat, had the most states. Of course President-elect Stevens had split the Republican vote, so that was to be expected."

"But then?"

"Well, eventually, even though the Lincoln Party hadn't run a single candidate for Congress, several Republican members gave rather stirring speeches in favor of Stevens. The speeches obviously had a serious effect. And, I might say, several small states with fewer members made a big difference. They ended up with Secretary, or should I say, President-elect Stevens."

"Well, thank you, sir. I'm sure we are all tired, but it's a relief to have a decision made."

"A relief it is!"

"Well, thank you Representative Robertson."

It was noon. Mark had had little sleep, but he was filled with energy. Both Christina and Rodney had called with their congratulations. Mark asked Rodney to be on the inaugural platform on the 20th. An excited Christina wanted to be with Mark a week before the 20th.

There were swarms of media outside of Mark's townhouse as the delegation of seven tired House members entered Mark's living room.

At Mark's invitation, the media crowded the room. Jorge served everyone catered coffee and sandwiches.

When the air of festivity calmed down, Republican House member Alan Smith of Tennessee, the senior member of the group, spoke. "Sir, it is my honor to report to you that the United States House of Representatives has selected you to be the next President of the United States of America. You will take the oath as President on January 20th at noon." He spoke with a slight Southern twang.

The entire room of people broke into applause. Mark, who was dressed informally, spoke. "Representative Smith, it is my honor to accept the House's decision. This has been a long and trying campaign. It is, at last, over and now is the time for action. As President I intend to lead this nation in its fight against terrorists. We shall find them and eliminate them, wherever they may be. As I promised in the campaign, that will be my first order of business. I want to assure Boston, and all those cities that have been attacked, that the government's efforts to rebuild the destroyed facilities will be quickly accomplished. I will answer a few questions."

"Sir, were you surprised at winning the Presidency?"

"Yes and no. As you will recall I was reluctant to run, but decided that I must get across my message about the terrorist threat. Unfortunately, the terrorists got that message across better than I did."

"Did you expect to win?"

"Certainly not when the campaign began, but the more I campaigned, the more I wanted to win. But, I admit, as a third party candidate running against a President under whom I served, I was not very optimistic."

Mark pointed at another reporter. He had not yet learned their names. "Sir, will you have any agenda other than the fight against terrorism?"

"Yes, I will. And I intend to outline the same in my inauguration speech and then my first address to the Congress."

"You will be the first bachelor President in many years. We know of your relationship with Christina Bagliani. Do the two of you expect to marry?"

Mark laughed. "Now you are getting very personal. Ms. Bagliani has a life and a very important and successful career of her own, but . . . I think I should leave that one alone.

"Thank you very much," Mark continued. "Now I think we all need some sleep before I put my foot in a bucket that I can't get out of. See you all January 20th."

The group laughed and slowly began emptying the room. Jorge closed the door when the last person had left.

Rolf smiled at his friend. "Well, what about you and Christina?"

Mark waived him off. "How the hell do I know?"

CHAPTER THIRTY

The Secret Service virtually surrounded Mark as he joyfully hugged Christina when she stepped from her plane. He would have to get used to the Secret Service and the TV cameras following his every move. There would be little privacy for the next four years.

"Congratulations, my darling," she said oblivious to the crowd as she and the President-elect embraced. "You did it. You'll be President of the United States in less than a week!"

"Are you as surprised as I am?" asked Mark as they sat in the black S.U.V. that would be his ground transportation as President. He was grinning broadly, holding her hand.

"No, I am not. But then, I don't understand your system of selecting a leader." Their vehicle waited for no traffic signals, nor traffic, as they sped to Georgetown.

The next morning, Mark and Christina were still in bed when he asked, "What are we going to do?"

"About what, my dear?"

"About us."

"What about us?" They had not gotten out of the large bed. Their hair was mussed and they were holding one another.

Mark propped his head with his hand. He loved to look at Christina's naked body. Maybe it was not as perfect as it was when their off-again and on-again affair began well over 30 years ago, but she was an exciting woman and he loved her, even more than then.

"As President, I think I need a First Lady and I think it should be you."

She was surprised by his words. He had asked her to marry him! "But, darling, I have my life in Rome." As when she was stressed, her accent was more pronounced.

"Listen, Christina Bagliani, I am to be President of the United States. Aren't I supposed to have my orders followed?" Mark had a joking lilt in his voice.

"I'm an Italian citizen. You cannot give me orders. It would cause an international incident." She playfully pushed his elbow out from under him and kissed him. "A woman needs time to think about such things. Let's have breakfast and talk about it." Despite the joking, her tone was serious.

In half an hour they were dressed in leisure clothes and sitting together in the breakfast area off the kitchen. Jorge had brought Christina her continental breakfast, while Mark had scrambled eggs and toast. Both had coffee.

"I think marriage would work," he said. "There are more and more married couples who live far apart and only see one another when they can. You can still have *Il Verita*. I know how important the newspaper is to you."

"Why can't we stay the way we are now? We love each other. Isn't that enough?"

"I want the world to know I love you. I want you to be my First Lady."

"But I would fly over when you need me. Like for formal diners. That sort of thing."

"Then you don't want to marry me?"

"It's not that I don't, but—" She started to cry, returning her croissant to its dish and putting her hands to her face.

He reached to her hand.

"Don't you see?" she asked. "It would mean giving up who I am after all these years of . . . well, becoming who I am now."

"But I need you to be mine."

"I am yours. There certainly will never be anyone else. But marriage . . . well marriage means more than occasionally seeing one another." Tears were still in her eyes. She dabbed them with her tissue.

Mark pulled his chair closer and leaned toward her. "Surely, we could work it out. As I say, other couples do."

She put her hand on his. "Perhaps some other time. Would you keep your offer open? Maybe someday I could just write editorials and not manage the newspaper."

"But even if we don't marry," he said. "You would come over as often as you could and be my First Lady?"

"Of course I would, my dear Mark. Of course I would." Her eyes were reddened, but she had put down her tissue.

Mark felt rebuffed. And sad. He remembered so many years ago when they rendezvoused in Paris. He had loved her so very passionately and she had returned that love, only to tell him that she planned to marry Bagliani. Bagliani was rich and the owner of Il Verita. Mark was only a penniless student at Oxford. Although his love had never died, he had never fully recovered from Paris.

But now was now and he would make the best of it.

It was January 20th. The Chief Justice led Mark through the President's oath of office. Setting a precedent, Christina stood at Mark's side. The Secret Service had insisted that the ceremony be in the Capitol Rotunda. The historic room was filled with dignitaries, including many members of Congress. The TV cameras were broadcasting the occasion to the world. Giant screens had been set up outside the Capitol to accommodate the crowds that stood in the cold weather.

"I do solemnly swear that I will faithfully execute the office of President of the United States and will to the best of my ability, preserve, protect and defend the Constitution of the United States."

Mark swallowed. He was President. He had only wanted to warn the country of the renewed terrorist threat, but a very long road had led to this momentous day. Would he be able to live up to the challenge? Last night he had tried to write out his inaugural address. He had thought of the best speeches. Lincoln's second inaugural. Roosevelt's "We have nothing to fear but fear itself." Kennedy's "Ask not what your country can do for you." But he decided that he was at his best when he spoke extemporaneously. He pushed his doubts aside and began his speech. His voice was firm and strong. He had written only a few notes.

"Americans, we face a challenge that we must win. There are terrorists in our midst. They will not be satisfied with blowing up our television stations to gain their evil ends. They will not be satisfied with blowing up our embassies abroad. In my forthcoming address to Congress I shall present specific proposals to deal with the terrorist cells within our borders and in other countries. I have no Congressmen and women pledged to me, but I expect to work with members of both parties to attack this problem. I demand action.

"I have many political views that are closer to those of my friends in the Democratic Party, but my views on economic matters are those of the Republican Party. I expect to work with the Congress to deal with these issues.

"But those matters aside, by far and away the most important issue is Tamar. Tamar is the head of the terrorism dragon. We shall decapitate the dragon at once. I now warn the King of Tamar that if Assad and his people are not removed from his island in ten days time, the armed forces over which I command will destroy them. If the King so requests I shall order the United States Marines to assist him. But I tell him now that at the end of ten days time I shall proceed regardless of the King's wishes." Mark briefly turned away and looked at the gathered Congressmen. "My message to all is clear, I will not tolerate the existence of the terrorist threat on the island Kingdom of Tamar. I know that I have the support of the American people in that endeavor."

The applause was more than polite, but not overwhelming. Perhaps, Mark thought, they realized the gravity of the situation. No matter the reason, Mark knew he would go forward with his plan against the terrorists.

Later, as he left the Capitol, he wished he had hired a professional speechwriter to write his speech. He was uncertain that he had gotten his message across.

Derek turned off the TV in Assad's tiny headquarters. "What do you think? Was he bluffing?" wondered Assad.

"Mark Stevens doesn't bluff." Derek's expression was grim.

"I'm going to stay here and fight," said Assad. "The King will never be able to force us out. I really don't care if the Americans kill us all. We'll kill as many as we can. I'll go down fighting.

* * *

"Where are we going?" asked Christina. They were in a caravan of Secret Service vehicles. Reporters and cameramen frantically followed.

"We're going to Monticello."

"Monticello?"

"Yes it's the home of Thomas Jefferson, our third President. When he was in his 30s, he authored Declaration of Independence. It declared the colonies independent from England."

"Oh. Why are were going there?"

"When I was Secretary of Treasury I used to drive there to do some thinking. I want to show it to you and besides I want to do some thinking about a decision."

"And what is that Mr. President?" Christina reached for Mark's hand.

"You'll see, my dear. You'll see."

Mark showed her the various rooms of the iconic mansion. He explained the history of Jefferson's designing the house and living there until he died. The Secret Service gave them as much privacy as they could, following at a respectful distance. They had asked the tourists to step aside.

"I find Jefferson's memory very inspiring."

"As I see this house and now that you've told me about Jefferson, I can see why."

They stepped outside to the graveyard. "I want you to see the grave marker. It's very special to me."

"All right, my dear."

They stood in front of the obelisk marker. "Please read the words," he asked.

She read aloud. "Here was buried Thomas Jefferson. Author of the Declaration of Independence, of the Statute of Virginia's Religious Freedom and Father of the University of Virginia.

"But I thought you said he was President."

"That's the point. He was President, but he deliberately left it off."

"Strange. Why?"

"I really don't know. I guess because the other accomplishments were more important to him."

"Hmm."

"You see that's what has got me to thinking."

"What?" she quizzed.

"Well, knocking out terrorism sooner than four years is really more important to me than being President. As to the other issues, I'm intending to reach an accommodation with Congress in those same four years."

"And if you don't? What's your point?"

"I'm not going to seek a second term. I saw what happened to Knox in his first term—and what happened to many other Presidents—they spend too much time setting the groundwork to get re-elected. I'm going to concentrate on the next four years. I'm not even going to think about a second term. I'm not going to be another power seeking guy like Knox."

"Are you going to announce that you're not going for re-election?"

"I don't think so. I don't want to turn into a lame duck in my first term and not accomplish what I want."

"A lame duck?"

"Yes, an American term. It refers to the fact that when everyone knows it's your last term in office, it's not easy to accomplish things."

"So you're not going to announce it?"

"No, I don't think so. I know I don't want to sit in the oval office vetoing bills and making speeches."

Christina sat puzzled on the trip back to the White House. Mark had always been an unconventional man. This decision seemed strange to her, but she guessed he knew what he was doing.

She and Mark spent one night in the family quarters of the executive mansion before she boarded her plane to

Rome. She thought about Mark's proposal of marriage as her jet circled around Washington for a glimpse of the White House before heading toward Rome. She had to admit that Washington was an exciting place and she pondered what it would be like to be married to Mark Stevens, President of the United States.

* * *

It was now the last day of the ten-day period of President Stevens' ultimatum to Assad and the King of Tamar. The King had met with Assad and insisted that he and his men leave the island.

It was of no avail. Assad's troops had stormed the King's palace, overpowered the ineffectual palace guard, and murdered the King.

Under Stevens' order a U.S. aircraft carrier stood within sight of the shore of Tamar. The Navy announced that tomorrow the base on Tamar and the airfield would be destroyed. Modern landing craft stood by for invasion.

Early that night Derek's plane took off and headed northwest toward Singapore. The U.S. Navy waited for dawn and the ordered military action. On board were Hardin's two pilots and his attractive female flight attendant. Derek was the only passenger. The flight attendant was in the rear, preparing diner.

Derek spoke softly only to himself. "If Mark Stevens thinks he's going to survive the next four years, he is very much mistaken. I'll see to that."

The U.S. aircraft carrier's modern radar system spotted Derek's plane as it left Tamar. The Captain ordered one of his supersonic planes to follow the jet, while he contacted the Pentagon.

"Mr. President," the Admiral was calling the White House from his post in the Pentagon. "Sir, a private jet has taken off from Tamar. We didn't want to shoot it down, without consulting you."

"Shoot it down," ordered President Stevens. "Yes, Shoot it down." Mark wondered if it might be Derek's plane. He very much doubted that Hardin would face the invasion of the Marines. The man would flee, if he possibly could.

The Commander of the U.S. jet had visual contact with Derek's plane when the order came through. "Shoot the bastard down!"

"Yes, sir," the pilot responded as he released his missile toward the fleeing aircraft.

The U.S. fighter circled the area to be certain the target had vanished into the ocean and then turned back toward his carrier. For a moment its Commander thought he saw what could have been a raft near the crash site. But he decided that he was mistaken. He thought that no one could have survived that crash.